A Deja View

An original para*Flix*® hybrid novel to movie by:

Ned Schwartz

2016

This is a book published by para*Flix*®
© 2015 by para*Flix*®

All rights reserved under International and Pan-American Copyrightconventions. Published in the United States by para*Flix*®

Port St. Lucie

With para*Flix*... It's OK to hear voices! ®and para*Flix* are a registered trademarks of para*Flix*®

www.para*Flix*.com

ASIN: B018ES5EVE

ISBN: 13-978-0-9972303-1-4

For Eli...

my past, our now, your future

A Deja View

What if all our memories, impressions, and life experiences are imprinted on our DNA? What if our subconscious connects with this... might this explain deja vu? What if we inherit our parents' DNA with all this information and it becomes part of our DNA?

A Deja View is a sci-fi journey into our DNA... involving past secrets, current threats, future jeopardy, payback and redemption relying on solving the mysteries of our DNA.

It is the 1990's and Edison Barr has a problem... from his father's past. Unfortunately, Edison never knew his father and doesn't even know if he died long ago or has been in prison his whole life, since his mother refuses to talk about him. A rather imposing dark and menacing figure believes that Edison is in possession of information regarding the whereabouts of a cache of uber rare double eagle gold coins, believed to be long lost since the 1930's. He is just now threatening Edison and his family for that information, supposedly left to him by his father.

As the threat becomes more clear and present, Edison is forced to engage in a very risky and questionable experiment to tap into his DNA as a means to access clues to his father's life prior to his own conception, in order to find out just what happened those many years ago, before he was even born... to neutralize the very real current threat against him, his partner, their newly born son and his silent mother.   These clues lead Edison on a trek of both geography and the heart while triangles of both intrigue and true love evolve before the 'truth' is uncovered and unraveled on the shores of Laupahoehoe, Hawaii, site of a devastating tsunami in the 1940's... bringing families from several walks of life to deal with the unspoken generational connection between father and son.

Follow Edison on his journey into his father's past, leading to his own current challenges, in order to protect his son's future.   We go back in time, not with a science fiction time machine, but through the unknown possibilities of our individual DNA.

CONTENTS

A Deja View

Chapter I

Back in the 60's

The frayed white satin drapes were nearly worn through. The old double hung window was so warped and covered with a dozen coats of paint, that once closed in the Fall, it wouldn't budge until Spring.

It was unusually warm for a March 16th in Springfield, Massachusetts and Artie wanted to open the window to air out the house from the indoor staleness lingering from a typically brutal New England Winter.

"Damn this window!" Artie murmured to himself, not looking forward to the effort it would take to open it and not possessing the strength of his youth any longer.

After straining to push the window up, Artie's delicate hands were shaking uncontrollably. He then leaned into the window with his shoulder pushing upward, trying not to break the glass… and after several attempts, finally the paint in the seams cracked open and a March breeze caused the curtains to flap in the wind as though there wasn't a care in the world. Artie took in a deep breath, rubbed his shoulder and smiled…he was relieved.

The living room was somewhat oversized for the small four-room bungalow, built some fifty odd years ago after the turn of the century. It showed its years of neglect, especially since the onslaught of the great depression and World War II. Money was needed for food and not luxuries, like fixin' up the house.

The sofa and chair were worn through the threads on the corners and arm rests. The throw carpet was curled up on the ends, but was regularly swept. The hardwood floors were warping out of shape and the papered walls peeled in the corners. There were a couple of pictures hanging on the wall from the Woolworth's five and dime.

The one exception was the dark brown mahogany Baldwin upright piano, in its prominent position between the kitchen and the bedroom. The crisp late winter air made the keyboard action especially quick, not that he needed any help from the weather. Artie 'Fingers' Clark was no stranger around the ivories and had the touch to pound out some of the most inspirational jazz and gut wrenching blues from those keys you'd ever want to hear. Artie needed to calm his hands.

It was a lazy day, and Artie was just gazing at his new three-month old son, perched in the corner of his crib, providing background music in the form of hiccups… in a syncopated pattern, true to his heritage, hiccup, hiccup... hiccup. It was an unusual scenario for Artie, a man of fifty something, with a gravely voice, crows feet around his eyes, a gray receding curly hairline… and large dark brown eyes. A face that reflected a hard life… the daily struggles faced by a black man in the first half of the twentieth century.

Artie survived… a result of his reservoir of talent, intelligence and shear stubbornness.

Artie was tinkering on the keyboard, fingering a combination of chord progressions with a riff of E, B B, E, A, E, B A, E Bflat7 sustained and started singing …

"... You got those hicci cup blues, don't knows what to dos, about them hicci cup bluuues . . . You've got them hicci cup bluues, don't knows whaaat to dos, about them hicci cup bluuuues.

Well I don't knows, I don't really cares... your mamma's got you wear'in cheap underwears, you got them hicci cup bluues, don't knows what to dos, about them hicci... those hicci cup bluuues…"

As he was beginning to move into the next verse and gaining some desperately needed momentum, his young wife called out from the other room, her voice just a bit too soft for the environment,

"Oh Artie, stop that fooling around and please bring baby to me. I haven't much time to get over to the 'X'. We need some food you know, and I must get to Gus and Paul's for some fresh bread for dinner tonight. It should be coming out of the oven in a few minutes. You know how Baby just loves the smell of fresh bread bakin."

"Oookey Dookey" he strained as he picked up his son, still hiccuping away, "Guess your mama wants me to get serious 'bout my music here!"

Artie carried his son out to the next room and came back and stared at the piano.

"We'll be back in an hour or so. Why don't you finish that tune you've been working on?"

"You mean those hicci cup blues?!"

"No, you old fool", she laughed playfully, in an intimate way, "you KNOW what I mean!" She gave him a peck on the check.

"Yehggm." Artie grumbled an unintelligible acknowledgment while he stroked his fingers briefly through her hair as she walked away. He then plopped down on the piano stool and spun around a full turn.

Before he could get his fingers back on the keyboard, another parting reminder from his bride,

"And I wish you wouldn't go out while we're gone. We don't need any more problems... you heard Detective Dugan... all the others... dead... murdered... and that monster getting parole last week."

Artie, tired of being constantly nagged, was quick in his response. "He's just a kid, wet behind the ears. He ain't gonna cause me no trouble, Momma." That was 30 years ago... Look around, you see any gold laying around here, ha?" "I got screwed just like he did."

"After spending years in prison, I doubt he's still wet behind the ears... and I don't think he's a kid any longer... and I don't think he knows or cares you got screwed, too... so just stay inside where it's safe, at least while we're gone, won't you?"

"OK, OK, yeah, don't worry."

As Artie heard the front door closing, he got up and stuck his head into a tin of Ritz crackers, fished for a couple broken crackers and opened a jar of nearly used up peanut butter and scraped the edges of the jar with the crackers pieces, then dipped them into an opened can of crushed pineapple, his favorite snack.

"Anything to avoid getting back to work", he thought to himself staring down the piano.

He glanced over to the kitchen table with the leftover dessert from last night, a Ritz cracker mock apple pie, a depression delicacy. Artie knew if he polished off the rest of the pie, he'd be in for it, so he dutifully stuck to the broken pieces left in the box, knowing that later, he could sweet talk his way to have that last piece, anyway.

Artie was lucky, having made the connections to scrape out a living cranking out piano tunes for a Boston player piano roll company whose corporate goal was to exploit down on their luck musicians for any non-copyrighted material it could get…cheap. The rolls would be sold to those would be musicians whose only talent is to control how fast to push the player piano pedals.

Artie was gazing into the keys of the piano, hearing the reflections of his life past and seeing the foundation for his future life. Artie knew that having his son so late in life was a time for introspection… and planning for his future… his son's future… their future, together for however long that would be.

"I gotta forget all the old crap, gotta make a future, now, can't give a shit 'bout all the assholes who are out to screw ya. My boy's gonna get a good education, make lot's of money, the right way…be a doctor or something…Dr. King gonna make it happen, yeah."

Still, he knew better, the realities of the bitter schism staring him in the face for most of his lifetime… at least until meeting his young bride.

Finally, things made sense. Finally, fifty years of overcoming the odds, knocking heads all alone and persevering when most men would have succumbed to the relentless societal drubbing . . . yeah, it finally made sense.

"I gotta get my boy everything I couldn't get….I got a good woman, a good momma… gotta get him into the best schools… gonna take a lotta hard work, but that's OK… not afraid of hard work…good books, good teachers, travel, yeah, lots of travel…gotta reach out and get to know the real people out there, oh yeah."

Artie was a truly gifted, yet generally unknown jazz and blues pianist unrecognized by the general public. Those in the know however, knew of Artie 'Fingers' Clark. Artie didn't have the flamboyance necessary to make it big in a white world. But the local honky tonks in New Orleans, Chicago and especially Pittsburgh knew Artie... knew him well. Pittsburgh was where he grew up, and the new generation of jazz musicians, like Harry 'the Slide' Barton, Johnny 'Good Vibes' Zimmer, 'Uncle' Johnny Walters and Louie 'The Lip' Pillson all got their start with Artie. They were his kids, his students, his family, along with the countless hundred others who picked up on music for the first time after sneaking in to listen to that 'Fingers' guy down on Liberty and Wylie Avenues.

But... to get by during those heady days, you didn't hang with future C.E.O.s, M.D.s or preachers.

Artie was good at everything he set his mind to. He was always known as the 'go to guy'. Always willing to help out a friend. If a friend needed to scrape together some scratch, Artie pitched in... for the spontaneous 'jams'... or other even shadier activities.

Artie had the touch... the magic fingers. He could identify any fabric with his eyes closed, merely by touch. Wool, cotton, blends, linen, denim, no sweat. Touching someone's face, he could sense the slightest increase in body heat, perspiration or nervous twinge. If you needed to know if someone was tellin' it straight, Artie was the man. His fingers were the human prototype to the polygraph lie detector. Yep, he was the man, alright. He could crack just about any safe faster than it took most people to open one with the combination.

Artie also had a memory like a steel trap, which today was a mixed blessing. His bride reminded him of that. The one job, thirty years ago, the one that took the most skill and daring, the one that could've been the home run, the one that could of set him up for life… the one that fell flatter that a pancake. Nothing. All for nothing!

So, it was the thinkable, the inevitable, the almost expected… that suddenly came hurling through that open window, framed by the flapping curtains… a tightly bundled cluster of dynamite sticks, connected to a burning fuse that looked like a sparkler from a the Fourth of July.

The fuse was far too short to do anything, yet long enough in its three remaining seconds for Artie to embrace his life in a burst of images… a collage of memories and emotions spewing out like a volcano. More importantly, it was a relative lifetime, to shed a single tear, as both a reflection of his religious repentance of the bitter mistakes of his past and even worse, a pain, that might only last but a final two seconds, yet had the intensity of ten generations of human endurance through struggles and repression, all vividly reflected wrinkles on Artie's face, knowing… yes, that gut wrenching kind of knowing… he would never see his son again… another tear… another remaining second... his only son, the only remnant of his life to survive, the hopes and dreams for a better life, wanting his boy to have all of life's opportunities that he never had… the overwhelming sadness of knowing he would not be there for him… and being a religious man, knowing he would not see his son again, until…

Epilog

The reporter in the *Springfield Morning Gazette* put it as succinctly as anyone could. He stated at the end of the article describing the total destruction of the home at 415 Morris Rd, "About the only logical thing to do at the site of the explosion, would be to construct a toothpick factory. They would have enough material for a long, long time."

Chapter II

The Case

Detective Ernie Dugan had one of those paunches that was a monument to all the doughnuts he inhaled at the squad room or on a stakeout. His stomach grew over his suit trousers like a glacier during the early stages of an ice age. More often than not, those cinnamon raisin fritters were the size of a candlestick bowling ball. They were Ernie's only salvation from the hanging stench of cigarette and cigar smoke... and the wafts of liquor lingering on too many breaths at the precinct.

His physique aside, Ernie belied the stereotype of an Irish precinct detective. Ernie didn't smoke or drink and was somewhat of a rarity among his colleagues. For that reason alone, Ernie was a bit out of the thick of it. Instead of going the Irish Keg Room after a shift for a bit of elbow bending with his colleagues, Ernie would stay at the squad room meticulously transcribing the day's activities into his case logbook, every minute detail being referenced to each pending case.

After that tedious daily chore, Ernie would go home. During the early years, when he was single, home was the boarding house, kept up by the widow Goldstock. She was very accommodating to Ernie. She would always have a hot meal waiting for him when he arrived, no matter when the others ate. She was just grateful to have a Springfield detective living there. It gave her a real sense of security.

After dinner, Ernie would read and re-read all of his notes and his logbook to make sure that no information was forgotten, no connection overlooked until falling asleep, often with his clothes on.

Later, after marrying his wife Nancy, he would not make it home on a typical day until long after dinner was back in the refrigerator, waiting to be re-heated into a dried out rubbery afterthought of its original presentation. Many days, his two children would already be in bed. It was the standing joke in the Dugan household that they should buy a mannequin from the Forbes and Wallace department store and leave it dutifully sitting at the dinner table.

Today was St. Patrick's Day and in Springfield, Massachusetts that meant no school for the kids and a light day at the precinct. This was the first day for Ernie's young son, Tom, to go to work with his father. This St. Patrick's Day also marked the 30th anniversary of Ernie's promotion to Detective on the Springfield Police force. Ernie and Tom both looked forward to this day when they could spend some quality father and son time together. Other than Sundays and holidays, time together was a scarce commodity.

It was a toss-up who was more proud, Ernie or Tom. There was a unique bond that morning, one that defied words or explanation… just a connection between a father and son where both, implicitly and without question, understood each other like no two other people on this planet could know each other. It was emotional for a man not comfortable dealing with his feelings. It was a day that would not only establish the bridge between two generations, but also seal the fate of a young son's future.

Ernie's roll top desk was still neatly organized with a growing number of file cabinets now flanking the desk, containing the copious notes taken on the hundreds of cases both solved and still pending. File folders were precisely stacked according to the case. Ernie's suit now accommodated both his police accoutrements and his expanding girth. Most importantly, the brown cork bulletin board was still there... with the same photos, the same schematics and the same newspaper blurbs, albeit yellowed and curled on the edges. But then again, it was 'The Case'.

Captain Dick Morgan was making his rounds through the squad room as he did every morning, but today, you could see that he was somewhat distracted, without focus on the daily procedures. This generally meant a short fuse. Time to stay away. Certainly, this was not the time to remind him of the big 30th anniversary. No time to introduce him to his son, Tom. Yet, without any attempt to engage the Captain, Ernie's body language somehow projected the pride he was experiencing at the moment and Morgan, must have somehow sensed this and eventually found his way to Ernie's desk.

"Ernie", he almost proclaimed, as though he was looking for someone to bail him out of his funk, "Busting 'em a little young today, are we?" as he motioned to Tom, sitting by Ernie's left side. "What heinous crime has this perp committed... armed robbery in a candy store with a loaded pretzel rod in his coat, or did he just play hooky from school? I hope to God that he's not your latest suspect in the Train Case?"

Tom, not being one to sit on the sidelines and not knowing this was the department Captain, immediately piped up.

"Hey, take that stuff back, I'm a straight A student and never played hooky a day in my whole life, you creep!"

The Captain knew he had met his match and muttered something about the apple never falling far from the tree and walked away.

Despite the moment, Tom knew something bad had happened when his father had his morning coffee with the paper at home. Ernie let forth a rare expletive when he read the front page about the big explosion the day before and crunched the paper that he usually kept in such pristine condition. One simple word,

"Damn!"

Tom wasn't sure what was going to happen today when they went down to the station. He was worried because this was their day and he didn't want it to be ruined by some unknown crook that might take away his dad from him on their day.

Ernie every so slowly and methodically pulled out a permanent black laundry marker and with the precision of a surgeon, etched an "X" across the photograph with the name of E. Arthur 'Fingers' Clark written below it. There were four similar pictures up on Ernie's brown corkboard and now, three of the four had been 'X'ed out along with Marcus Winston and Benny Weiss. The sole remaining picture was one Harry 'Hacksaw' Elam. Ernie tapped the marker on the desk for several moments, slowly shaking his head. It was the look of a man knowing exactly what was going on, but without the power to do anything about it... pure frustration. He knew there would be renewed activity on The Case when Elam was released from prison last week, but he never expected this.

As Tom would find out later, this was the day that Ernie started losing all hope that someday The Case would finally be solved... and the stolen gold $20 double eagles recovered.

Somehow, Tom sensed this and asked a simple but cathartic question of Ernie,

"Hey dad, how come you're crossing out those pictures?"

All the factors of the day surfaced. The 30th anniversary of working on the same case, Tom finally being old enough to understand police work, and the explosion from the day before. It is now time to let young Tom know what his dad has been doing these past years. Now is the time for his son to understand all the lost time with his father because he was working on... The Case.

"I need to tell Tom everything." Ernie thought.

Chapter III

The Heist Man Trophy

Ernie landed his detective badge thirty years ago. He was a fanatic over the details of every case he was assigned. It was this ability to sweat the details he kept in his logbook that got Ernie his big break; out of the uniform and into the suit.

That first morning in the detective squad room, three decades ago was the proudest moment of his life. Having his own desk, his own nameplate, even his crisp new dark blue worsted wool double-breasted suit reflected the newness of his job. The gun holster on his left side and the badge wallet in his breast pocket revealed the telltale signs of a rookie detective who bought his first suit without taking into consideration these accoutrements to his job. Ernie was even oblivious that morning as the veteran detectives all came by his desk, one by one and patted him dutifully on the bulges, snickering while welcoming him to the squad room. The high achieved that morning would be unceremoniously offset by the years of angst and frustration over the very first case he would be assigned as a rookie detective later that same day. The Case.

"Well, Tom, let me tell you about these pictures. It was a cool St. Patrick's Day, thirty years ago. Most of the detectives left for the Keg Room before lunch for the holiday festivities, and most of the uniformed cops were assigned to parade duty, which started at noon, down by the railroad station on the corner of Lyman and Main Streets, you know, down by the Paramount. After the Mayor's speech, the parade proceeded down Main Street to the South End, just past where the Red Rose is today."

"I was alone in the squad room at 12:18, eating lunch at my desk and organizing my stuff. Suddenly, Tony Marcuso, one of the senior detectives on the squad, I don't think you ever met him, came running in and grabbed his coat and started to run out as quickly as he ran in. I never realized how one fateful second, being in the wrong place at the wrong time... well anyway, Tony saw me and yelled, 'Come on kid, it's time you got your feet wet.' I remember that moment... like it was last week."

"Tony quickly described the situation to me. Apparently a gang of at least four, maybe more, held up a train coming into the station, right where the parade started, with all those people around... can you believe it? Apparently, nobody paid any attention to where the parade started, I mean, everyone was watching the parade going down Main Street... pretty smart actually. Anyway, you know the railroad trestle that goes over Main Street and heads to the train terminal on Lyman Street, perpendicular to Main?"

"Yeah, sure," said Tom.

"Well, that trestle is about a thirty yards across Main Street and about 14 feet high over the street. As a courtesy, the 11:55 coming from New York and Philadelphia en route to Boston held about a hundred yards down track until the parade got going."

"Then, after the parade began, at precisely 12:09, the train proceeded over the trestle at a snail's pace to keep the noise down. Unbeknownst to the passengers on the train, the Philadelphia mint had shipped a box of recently minted 1933 double eagle $20 gold coins for storage... to both the New York and the Boston Federal Depository Branches. Each depository was to receive a box about two feet by one foot by 10 inches each containing 1,000 coins, weighing approximately 35 pounds. The delivery to the New York Depository went without any notice, but unfortunately, the shipment to Boston never made it to its destination."

"How come?" asked Tom.

"Well, as the transport car carrying the coins in a safe was in the middle of the trestle, a robber jumped along the conductor and slammed on the brakes."

The conductor barked, "What the hel... aah heck do you think you're doing?"

"Come on, don't sweat it, the Mayor doesn't want any more noise interfering with the parade." The gang member smoothly told the conductor.

"Well, shoot, all someone had to do is ask... for crying out loud." The conductor complained.

"No one else on board really paid much attention as they were squinting to see the end of the parade moving south and since the train was barely moving. Anyway, no one realized or cared that the train even stopped, they were all happy to see the parade.. Most everyone actually thought the conductor was just being accommodating, so everyone could enjoy a glimpse of the festivities."

"Meanwhile, two other members of the gang jumped the sole guard in the transport car, which cleverly opened on the opposite side of the parade where everyone was looking. Then one of them, allegedly one E. Arthur 'Fingers' Clark proceeded to crack the safe in the corner of the boxcar. He's the one there who just got 'X'ed out. Ernie stated, pointing to Clark's photo.

"Does that mean he got rubbed out?" Tom asked enthusiastically.

"I'm afraid so, Tom… he was killed in the explosion yesterday, down by the river."

"How come, if the robbery took place so long ago… and how come he's not in jail?"

"Well, there was never enough evidence to convict him… anyway, back to the story…the entire robbery ran like clockwork… just a couple minutes from beginning to end. Gotta give 'em credit for that, at least. Lucky for me, the second gang member in the transport car decided to steal the wallet, watch and ring from the security guard while 'Fingers' opened the safe and lowered the small crate of coins along with the wallet, watch and ring to the fourth gang member, the wheel man, waiting below on Main street in the getaway car on the north side of the trestle. Within three minutes, the train was robbed and made its way into the Lyman Street station while the getaway car with four people got away going north on Main toward Chicopee, at least according to the witnesses we interviewed. I think he's (pointing to Clark's picture) the one who masterminded the robbery… he was the only one smart enough to plan it so well."

"The conductor wasn't even sure what happened... other than being coerced to brake for a couple minutes on the trestle. After the conductor pulled in the station and walked back to the transport car, he found the guard tied and gagged. He immediately untied the guard to find out what happened and stopped the only police officer at the station. He called in the robbery to the police station and Tony and I raced over to the station to find out what happened."

Chapter IV

Tell Me a Story, Dad

"Those pictures are the people I think robbed the train, Tom," Ernie confessed, "and I've never been able to convict them or recover the gold coin shipment. I'm certain the ones with the X's have all been killed by the other guy, pointing to the remaining picture without an X over it."

Tom then asked "Who's the guy without the 'X' on it?"

Ernie said, "That son, is Harry 'Hacksaw' Elam. Harry was the wheel guy for the robbery." That means he was driving the getaway car. We caught him shortly after the heist and convicted him for the robbery after he tried to sell the stolen watch and ring from the train guard, but we never found the double eagle gold coins."

"Wow, how come they call him Hacksaw?"

Ernie was more than willing to tell Tom, knowing his son's penchant for scary stories.

"Well, the story goes that after the robbery, he was playing poker in jail one night and one of the players lost and owed Harry a lot of money. When Harry asked the guy for the money, he said he didn't have any. The guy was wearing a pinky ring and Harry said he would take that and settle the score. The guy said no.

Harry had a broken hacksaw blade he had been using for three years trying to cut his way out of his cell. He took out the hacksaw blade and asked if the guy would reconsider.

He said no. Harry then grabbed the other guy's wrist, held it down and gave the guy a stare, which told him in no uncertain terms that he was about to lose the pinky ring, along with the pinky."

"As the story goes, Harry got the ring and the finger and the guy needed nothing but Harry's stare as an anesthetic. The guy didn't flinch. It was his stare, not his surgical skill. From then on, Harry was called 'Hacksaw'. He ended up doing an additional 15 years for that incident. Hacksaw was one angry guy. Matter of fact, he just got out of prison a few weeks ago."

Tom piped up quickly, showing his knack for detective work like his old man,

"Did he knock off the guy you just crossed out in the picture?"

Ernie chuckled, "Tom, my boy, you ask too many questions."

"No, really, did he?" Tom persisted.

"I'd bet my last dollar on it, son, but don't tell your mother I said that."

"OK dad, that'll be our secret.   How are you going to get him?"

"I'm not sure Tom, but if it's the last thing I do, I'll get him and anyone else from that train robbery." "Besides, there's a 10% finders fee if I can recover the double eagles."

"How much is that, dad?"

"A lot of loot, son, a lot of loot. Could be a million bucks."

"You mean we'd be like the Millionaire on TV?"

"Well, I guess it would be, Tom." Ernie could see that an impression had been made on Tom and that is was time to change the subject. Ernie took Tom to the lab downstairs and then out for lunch at the Steiger's tea room. Ernie loved the biscuits there and knew Tom would love them, too.

Chapter V

Home Run Derby

[MONTHS LATER]

It was a warm sunny day for the annual Father's Day Home Run Derby at Plumtree Park. All of the Little Leaguers got their chance to become the next junior Babe Ruth with all the bragging rights and most importantly, the biggest, baddest trophy anywhere.

"C'mon Pop, give me a big ol' watermelon right over the plate, right here!" exhorted Tom pointing with his finger waist high. "I'm gonna to send this one to the moon!"

"CRACK". The ball sailed ten feet over the left center fence and the crowd went crazy. "Way to go Tommy boy!" Ernie yelled.

"That's my brother!" "Sign him up!" "Thar she blows!" all came from the crowd.

Tom beamed, after hitting his fourth homer to take the lead.

Home Run Derby was the traditional kick-off to the Little League season, where all the boy's fathers served up the most perfect pitches possible to allow their sons the best chance to clock one over the fence. The boy in each age bracket who got the most home runs in ten swings would get the trophy and a free twin skyscraper ice cream cone from Mike's Ice cream shop.

"Next up, Willieeeee Marshalllll!" crowed the announcer. Willie Marshall slowly walked up to the plate, his head hung down.

"Don't worry Willie, I've been practicing all week."

"Oh, ma, this is really embarrassing!" offered Willie.

The first pitch missed the plate by at least 3 feet. Willie put his hand over his eyes muttering,

"Can we just go home?"

"I'll do better this time, honey." soothed his mother.

"Right." Whispered Willie.

... And she did do better, this pitch only missed the plate by two feet. Willie was mortified. The third pitch sailed above his head and Willie wildly swung trying to at least make contact to end this embarrassment. He finally made contact, sending the ball dribbling down the first base line.

"Hang in there Willie!" could be heard from the adult crowd, but some of the other kids weren't so kind.

"Sign her up.... for the other team!" "Incoming... duck!" Willie wasn't having any part of this.

"Ma, you throw like a woman!"

Normally, his best friend Edison would be razzing him no end, but not this time. His turn was next.

One of the other fathers finally walked up to Willie's mom and asked if she wanted some help. She quickly agreed, but surprisingly, Willie protested coming to her rescue yelling,

"Hey, my mom can handle this, leave her alone!" After all, he was the man of the family, now.

She finally tossed an underhand ball close to the plate and Willie connected, drilling it over the left field fence.

"Hey, that's cheating," several of the boys chanted, "no fair!" "You can't pitch underhand."

"Let 'em be." "Give the kid a chance." and "You can do it." could be heard from the crowd.

One more underhand toss and Willie nailed it down left field line. Two homers, but Willie was still mortified.

Meanwhile, Edison was feeling his pain... before he even got up to the plate. He knew his mom hadn't practiced at all. He knew his mom wasn't as athletic as Willie's mom. It was bad enough that everyone was calling him Mr. Ed, from the TV show of the same name, imitating the horse call of "Whoa.... Willbur!" Now, in a matter of seconds, he would soon be facing an identical fate, but even worse.

This was one reason Willie and Edison were best friends. They just looked at each other, knowingly, as Willie walked away from the plate. They said nothing as they passed each other. Their sunken eyes said it all. The end of the world was surely upon him. Both fatherless and embarrassed... he truly loved his mother... but could it get any worse, especially on Father's Day with no father?

"Now batting, Edisonnnnn Barrrrr!"

CHAPTER 6

Pooling Your Assets

[THIRTY YEARS LATER]

Melissa Stone was in a state of suspense. Actually, she was experiencing neutral buoyancy in a twelve foot deep olympic swimming pool at the local JCC campus. She was hooked up to a borrowed air tank, flippers, a diving mask, snorkel and a light-weight belt loosely buckled under her seven-month pregnant belly. Mel's dirty blonde wavy hair was flowing in the water and her tan lines looked as though she had recently spent some time in Florida. She was wearing a men's large tee shirt over her bathing suit, while breathing normally, albeit somewhat unnaturally, looking for some moral support from her significant other, Edison Barr. Mel was continuously complaining about the extra weight she was carrying and Edison brought her to a scuba lesson so that she could get some relief for a few minutes in the pool.

Edison was distracted by his best friend, Will Marshall who was breathing erratically and nervously expulsing spurts of air, which enveloped his short afro haircut giving him somewhat of an angelic look under water. Edison laughed uncontrollably at Will's apparent uneasiness. Edison already had his C card and was comfortably maneuvering his six-foot two frame in the vicinity of about four other first timers with his dark wavy hair flowing in the water.

Kate, Mel's co-worker from the research lab was closely watching the three of them in the middle of the deep end of the pool, as this was not her first lesson. She wanted to make sure Mel was OK and not under any undue stress, breathing through a regulator and all.

Mel was breathing easily now and enjoying the respite from gravity. After several moments of failing to get Edison's attention, she shot a rather hard look at Edison through her facemask, as though to say, "Hello... like we're the one's having a baby together, what the hell are you doing paying attention to your buddy, who I really can't stand, when I'm here by myself!"

Will caught a glimpse of Mel through the rising air bubbles and rolled his eyes ever so slightly and Edison turned and immediately realized he'd better pay some attention to her.

After several more minutes, the instructor had everyone get out of the pool and take off the equipment.

"Why do I have to leave now, I was just starting to enjoy this." Mel whined.

"Time's up and the instructor needs his equipment back... don't worry, we can come back next Tuesday." Edison tried to console her.

Kate came over and worked with Edison, still in the pool trying to help Mel safely get out of the pool."

"Christ, I feel like a beached whale!" Mel made sure everyone heard as she struggled to get to her feet poolside.

Edison turned and saw Will ready to lose his lunch, so he swam out and guided him to the ladder and waited until he got out of the water.

Will shook his head a couple times to get the water out of his hair and ears and methodically took off all the equipment and placed it on the bleachers with the rest of the gear provided by the instructor.

Will pulled Edison aside on the way to the men's locker room, "Everything OK?"

"Yeah, same old stuff, she's OK. I hope it's just the hormones."

"Is she doing the pickle and ice cream thing, yet?

"Please, you computer geeks are so cliché... but believe it or not, she does want me to pick up a few things at the grocery store on the way home, do you mind... otherwise I'll..."

"Don't sweat it, I'll get a couple things myself."

"Fine, I think Mel came with Kate, so..."

"Doesn't matter, remember, I'm supposed to check on that shut down virus on your computer, so I have to go over to your place anyway."

"Oh, yeah, I almost forgot."

"Well, Mel didn't, she's been bugging me all night... no pun intended."

"Right... thanks." Edison imparted to Will.

"Did you feel any pressure while in the water?" Kate asked on the way into the Women's locker area. "Just concerned about the baby."

"Everything was fine, you don't have to worry so much, remember, I'm the doctor, here. I'd know if there was a problem." Mel stated rather clinically.

"Are you going to take a shower here or wait until we get to your place?" Kate asked.

"I'd better take a quick rinse here and get rid of the chlorine smell... there won't be much time when we get home. I hope to hell that the stupid caterer has everything set up by now." "Will you watch my stuff?"

"Sure, no prob." Kate assured her.

CHAPTER 7

Big Brother and the Holding Company

Edison enjoyed wandering around the supermarket. The shelves of food were like a playground for him. He loved to cook and was constantly on the prowl for the next secret recipe or food item to perpetuate his somewhat famous one pan, one plate one utensil easy cleanup meal. This is why Edison and Will got along as roommates at Mass State. Edison loved to cook, Will didn't and was perfectly OK with cleaning up. Edison's favorite book at the time was 101 Ways to Prepare Ground Meat.

All this would probably explain his near addiction for pizza. The permutations of the various toppings were endless. The five food groups were proportionately represented and the clean up was minimal. Yes, the perfect food. Tonight was not a pizza night however. Having already eaten a late lunch, he was more in the mood for snacking, so he picked up his favorites.

When he got to the check out registers, he did his quick analysis of which lane to get into… and ultimately chose lane 2, since there were no women in line holding their checkbooks with pen in hand. All the food of the patrons ahead of him appeared to have bar codes, so he was relieved that there would be no price checks slowing up the works.

Will showed up with a hand basket with a couple items and lined up behind Edison.

"Just throw your stuff with mine." Edison offered.

"I think I can afford to pay for my own food." Will advised.

"No, come on, you're fixing our computer and besides, it'll save time."

"All right, but I'm buying lunch next time."

"Fine, here... just throw everything here and we'll separate it later at the house."

The checkout cashier was a pleasant enough young woman with the name tag announcing that she was 'Jessica', a fact that Edison pegged her for a gen X'er. She was somewhat surprisingly friendly when she offered what sounded like a more than scripted, "Hi, how are you tonight?"

Edison had this effect on women. He seemed to project some aura of intelligence without being too geeky. This gentle confidence in his understated appearance and clothing made for a comfortable interaction with most people.

As Edison placed his items on the conveyor, Jessica somewhat playfully announced each product as she scanned it.

"Do you have a Big D Express Savings shopper card?" She inquired.

Edison pulled out the discount shopper's card, hoping for the holy grail, that he actually purchased an item which would generate a huge savings.

"One jar of Vlasic Pickles, one fudge swirl ice cream... you wouldn't be pregnant would you?..."

"See, I'm not the only one!" Will observed. "So much for clichés."

[MEANWHILE]

The room was dimly lit. It was a smallish den in a fairly modern garden style condo. There was a brand new Dell desktop computer, so marked on the mid tower sitting on the floor, with a 19 inch LCD flat screen computer monitor sitting on a computer desk, currently displaying various window databases, each in its separate corner on the screen. The Windows program was running along with the Netscape browser, all connected to a new cable modem so there was an always on connection to the internet. The equipment was top shelf stuff and the most powerful available. The room and walls were decorated (plastered actually) with pictures, lists and diagrams. The operator had been dozing off intermittently when a series of three beeps startled him, whereupon he immediately clicked his mouse to expand one of the databases to the full screen.

In the upper left had corner, the source was identified as the Big D in Springfield with the following items being displayed on screen:

Vlasic Pickles, half sour 20 oz	1.69
Ben and Jerry's Fudge Swirl 1 pint	2.18
Progresso Pizza Sauce 12 oz	1.58
Motts Applesauce 40 oz	1.74*
Heinz Ketchup 24 oz	2.11*
Green Pepper	.49
Yellow Onions	.79
Thomas English Muffin 6 pack	1.69*
Nabisco Vanilla Wafers 22 oz	1.80*
Ocean Spray Cranberry Juice 30 oz	1.55
Borden's Vanilla Ice Cream	2.49*
Nestle Butterfinger 2 oz	.50*
Ritz Crackers, 14.5 oz	1.89*
Skippy Red Fat Peanut Butter 20 oz.	2.44*
Dole Crushed Pineapple 32 oz	.89*

The items with asterisks were blinking with the following notation of the bottom of the screen...

ITEMS MATCHED...   009
COMBINATIONS...   003
PROBABILITY QUOTIENT   91%

He pulled out a notebook containing lists of foods and pounded his fist on the desk and half yelled,

"Unfuckin' real!" followed by clenched fist and an exuberant "Yes!"

* * *

Will was handing the food to Edison who bagged everything in order to get out of there as quickly as he could.

Jessica provided him with the obligatory,

"Thank you for bagging."

Edison used his remote control fob to open the blue Mazda MPV he just bought in anticipation of the new addition.

Will, after plopping into the passenger's seat, glanced at his watch, paused and asked, "Would you mind stopping by the post office so I can mail in my tax returns?"

"Aah, it's like April 15th, you haven't filed yet?"

"Nah, don't want to be too ahead of the curve... usually I wait until midnight... they usually have a great party going on at the post office... free food, music, people.... Great time."

"It's like 8 o'clock, we don't want to be too early do we?"

"It's all in the timing Edison, you should know that." observed Will.

There was a postal employee standing out in the middle of Liberty Avenue collecting returns as cars drove by, stuffing them in a large canvas bag, sort of like an IRS Santa.

As they drove toward Edison's place, they passed a DQ and Will and Edison looked at each other as they have done countless times since childhood... and both yelled out in unison, "Blizzard time!"

Will and Edison must have consumed thousands of Blizzards together over the years, starting when they were both grad students at Mass State during all nighters getting ready for orals and researching their dissertations. Will was getting his Ph.D. in Computer Information Systems, while Edison was getting his Ph.D. in Biogenetic Research.

Will offered, "Let's hold it to a small one tonight, OK?"

"What, you on some kind of diet?"

"Nah, just want to get working on your computer before it gets too late."

"Yeah, like it'll take you all of five minutes to figure it out."

"Well, you never know."

"Like when has it taken you more that five minutes to fix anything on a computer?"

"These new worms arc getting brutal..."

"I've never seen anyone working a keyboard at warp speed like you."

"Two Butterfinger Blizzards" Edison ordered.

"What size?" asked the clerk.

"Small, please."

"Do you want to eat them here? Edison asked.

"How 'bout we do 'em on the way." Will responded.

"Jeez, are we getting freakin' old or what?"

"Hey, you're the one with the kid on the way."

After listening to the whirring mixer machine whip up the vanilla soft serve ice cream with the mixed in crushed up Butterfinger candy bar, they collected their just desserts and headed over to Edison's.

CHAPTER 8

It's my party

Edison and Melissa were currently living in a moderately upscale rented condo in downtown Springfield, but were planning on purchasing a larger house somewhere in the suburbs after the baby was born. Melissa was adamant about finding a place in Longmeadow, an upscale bedroom community to the south of Springfield. Edison was a bit more ambivalent and was uneasy about the pretentious lifestyle there, but was willing to chance it due to the good reputation of its school system.

Edison parked in the underground lot and asked Will,

"Would you stuff the cups in the trash over there. If Mel finds out we stopped for Blizzards, she'll be pissed."

Edison and Will each carried a bag of groceries and took the elevator up to the 3rd floor. Edison juggled his keys and awkwardly opened the door to the apartment with one hand as the other was trying to keep food from falling out of the thin plastic grocery bags.

The entry area was dark and Edison assumed that Melissa was already in the bathroom. After taking about two steps in the foyer, the lights popped on and about ten people jumped from behind the furniture and yelled...

"SURPRISE!" and "HAPPY BIRTHDAY!"

Edison was truly shocked since Melissa was not generally one to engage in surprises. She had already given him a card and new Tag Heuer watch earlier that morning, so he wasn't really expecting anything like this. The living and dining rooms were decorated with the typical birthday banners available at the local party store and the tables were piled high with all types of munchies and other snacks like the puffed pastry hors d'oeuvres from COSTCO, celery and carrot sticks along with broccoli florets and green peppers with a creamy poppy seed dip.

Edison was experiencing mixed emotions. On one hand he was pleasantly surprised that Melissa would actually put herself out for such a party, but on the other hand, he was tired and was not looking forward to being the focus of a party. He was also fearful that they would prevail upon him to play his guitar and have some lame sing-a-long karaoke thing with Mel's co-workers.

Edison owned a music store in downtown Springfield on Chestnut Street, named Big Notes. He sold guitars, keyboards, harmonicas, school instruments, CDs and sheet music… but mostly, he was known for his unparalleled genius in creating custom electronic amplifiers, enhancements and mixers for guitars, string instruments and keyboards.

His clients were some of the most successful studio musicians in the world and some of the biggest name rock stars who were looking for that ever elusive 'new' sound. Rock, folk, country, R&B, even classical…they all came. On any given day a star might stop by unannounced to see Edison. His employees were amazed that such notable musicians would make a pilgrimage to Springfield, Mass., of all places. He made sure however, that they did not make a big deal of it, in order to preserve the privacy of his elite clientele. Although dozens of 'A' list music icons would visit Edison, there were no autographs and no pictures on the wall like those plastered all over the famous delis in New York.

This fact alone is why his reputation has spread throughout the music world. It is a rare commodity in the industry to have someone with both a real talent, and the discreet ability to work it without the hoopla and paparazzi associated with these famous people. It was also the only way he could service a variety of performers who were highly competitive and paranoid about insuring the secrecy and uniqueness of their 'sound'.

Edison had a real talent for identifying the natural sound and style of a musician and enhancing it with a subtle but effective and distinct tweak, always pushing the envelope just a nudge. Edison always had the desire to be a performer, but didn't quite have in innate talent to pull it off. His mother forced him into taking piano lessons growing up, but he never took to it and rather enjoyed the guitar more.

Fortunately, only one or two of the people at the party were aware of Edison's brush with the famous. In fact, even Melissa was only aware that he only had some important customers, but he was so protective of his real client's privacy that he never told her about them. She had no interest in music so Edison figured she wasn't really missing anything.

Will was aware of Edison's work because he frequently consulted with Edison about new developments in computer electronic generated music and software and shared the inside info with Kate, whom he had a soft spot for. Edison cornered Will shortly after getting there,

"There is no virus worm in our computer, is there? Edison queried.

"Aaah… maybe ." He hesitated.

"Don't maybe me, Mel put you up to this, didn't she."

"Actually, it was Kate."

"Well, since you're here, you're not getting off that easy."

"Say what?"

"Would you check out a mortgage company on the web for me… I need to find some qualifying financing for a house in Longmeadow, in case we start looking over the weekend."

"No sweat," Will readily agreed. "I'll check out the Web to see what's the best deal from the mortgage brokers and banks."

"Thanks." Edison said grabbing Will around his shoulders and patting him on the back.

Will and Edison had been good friends since childhood. Later, when they took different paths to college, the two found themselves together again as Ph.D. students at Mass State, even though they were in different departments... Will in Computer Science and Edison in Microbiology. They both found their way back in Western Massachusetts after taking entry level jobs in different cities. Will later landed a promising career position in the emerging computer/actuary field with the Mass Mutual Insurance Company and Edison just finally felt that Western Mass was home.

Edison had traveled extensively throughout the U.S. In fact, he has been to every state except Alaska and Oklahoma. But other than possibly working and living in the pacific northwest or the research triangle in North Carolina, he always felt that Western Massachusetts was home. Whenever he would be driving home from anywhere, Edison always marveled at the beauty of the Berkshires coming back on the Mass Pike. That's where it just felt right. That's where they both felt like home, so it was no surprise that the two of them, like brothers found their way back home.

CHAPTER 9

Mixing It Up

Melissa was working the room with her usual finesse, showing everyone the new Tag Heuer gold watch she gave Edison, while Kate was managing the food and drinks for the small crowd along with Cindy, the caterer who organized all the food.

Watching Kate, Edison realized that she was behind the party, and not Mel. "Yeah", he thought, "If Melissa had done all this there would've been sushi, patè and California rolls. "

Edison walked over to Kate, and lightly held her right elbow momentarily.

"Thanks."

Kate realized that Edison got it, and smiled.

Most of Melissa's lab research team was there, including Julie, Hank and Dave, along with a few friends and neighbors. The party quickly evolved normally, with small groups forming and discussions taking place in total exclusion to the others.

Edison was enjoying the hors d'oeuvres and mixing his traditional soda concoction of ½ Diet Coke and ½ Sprite, while others, except Melissa, were drinking beer and wine.

Kate noticed this and playfully inquired,

"Are you indecisive… or just weird?"

Edison just laughed and told her,

"I'm hedging my bet, between rotting my teeth out and ending up like the Canadian lab rats with cancer from too much artificial sweeteners.

"Sounds like a little of both." Kate responded.

Edison shot back,

"If I have to make a choice... I'll opt for the weird, then."

While Melissa was hobnobbing with the neighbors, Edison was surrounded by her research team at the buffet table. They were debating the efficacy of various strategies for having their lab rats absorb the 'test material' prior to re-introducing them to their learning test mazes.

Edison knew from his discussions with Melissa that the group was engaged in testing lab rats in mazes. They were trying to establish the means and methodology of learning and memory.

They would have several rats learn first-hand to work their way through a complex maze to find the ultimate goal, the prized piece of cheddar cheese. They insured that all the maze pathways were twice as tall as a rat standing on its hind legs. The team would first test a group of rats and carefully measure and benchmark their performance under varying conditions. They would later test the progeny of the first group of rats, in various permutations, to see if there was any 'knowledge' or 'experience' that might possibly have been inherited by the next generation... in the same maze conditions. Time after time, they found that indeed, the second and succeeding generations improved marginally over their ancestors. They were disappointed that the incremental improvement was small and dismissed the performance data as statistically insignificant.

They were now focused on what they euphemistically called the 'new material'. They were hoping for a dramatic improvement in the second generation using this 'new material'. Currently, the 'new material' was actually a euphemism for the ground up brains of the first generation rats after they died. They were hypothesizing that the progeny would ingest the gray matter of their ancestors and that the knowledge learned would be represented in the chemical compounds and find its way into the progeny's brain and chemically interact to integrate with the existing consciousness of the second generation.

The debate currently going on was should they merely allow the rats to ingest the 'new material' through normal feeding or should it be injected intravenously. They were studying the efficiency probabilities of the alternative methods.

Hank was concerned with the levels of intracellular calcium in the lining of the rat's stomach to facilitate the absorption through the lining into the bloodstream, while Julie was advocating using the most direct route to the brain, thereby minimizing possible degradation of the new material's potency.

Edison politely listened to their observations and after he had heard enough of unsupported conjecture, couldn't help but comment,

"I might suggest an alternative approach. Instead of introducing an external material component into the bloodstream, or indirectly through digestion, why not concentrate on identifying the progeny's targeted existing DNA, which would be genetically passed on directly and in-tact by their ancestors, especially if the both parents are involved in the primary maze exercise. "Access, think access, the solution is in identifying the DNA, the end game, not the conduit alternatives."

Edison ever so slowly eased away from the group to talk a bit more with Will and to glance back to assess the impact of his observation.

The group of researchers suddenly tightened up and the voices lowered to a loud whisper. They were quietly shaking their heads, rubbing their chins when a couple controlled snickers cut loose after assessing the unmitigated gall of a music store owner making such a suggestion on sophisticated cognitive research.

Dave, however, developed a slightly glazed look over his eyes, as if to ask himself,

"That was just so bizarre…could there be something to this?"

Kate just lightly smiled and gently nodded her head, more out of amazement and admiration. She sensed that there was more to Edison than she had learned about him through Melissa. Melissa had always characterized Edison as a nice guy, but someone without much in the way of ambition or intellect, so Kate took the opportunity to bring Melissa back into the group by asking her how they had met. The question was timely in order to change the tenor of the group's conversation.

Melissa was more than happy to oblige.

"Well, we actually met in Hawaii of all places… at the Honolulu Symphony Fun Run charity road race." "I was there for a conference, it was around Easter…I had just finished the race and was looking for some Gatorade… it was a really warm day and I needed to replenish my potassium and electrolytes… when this gorilla came up to me." (waving her finger, pointing at Edison)

"Edison doesn't look that hairy Mel," observed Kate.

"No, no… She's right!…I was wearing a gorilla costume from the CBS prop department… actually it was the same gorilla suit used by Tom Selleck in an episode of Magnum P.I." Edison added, "my brush with fame!"

"Anyway," groaned Melissa eyeing Edison for interrupting her story, "this gorilla comes up to me and nods and puts out his hand to shake with me. Like an idiot, I shake the gorilla's hand and then he pulls his hand away leaving me literally holding the gorilla's hand. And… you won't believe this… get this… all this sweat and perspiration from inside the gorilla's hand dumps into my cup… and almost fills it… there must have been four hundred milliliters!"

"And here I thought he was just going to give you a banana!" Will laughed.

"Hold on… that came later." Melissa added.

"So what did she say? Asked Kate.

"I expected she was this hot, but pretty dumb blonde valley girl type and would say something like, "Ycchh, or That is like…so gross, or what are you, some kind of lamo sicko." Edison explained. "But she really surprised me. She calmly observed, 'What exactly do you expect me to do with this diaphoresis fluid… it may have large concentrations of water, sodium and chloride, but only traces of potassium… I need potassium, you big ape.' "Well, when I heard that… I don't know about her, but I was hooked."

"Melissa chimed in, "Well, he put his hand back on, threw up his hands and walked away without beating his chest without so much as a grunt."

"That was it?" Dave asked.

"No... about a half an hour later, I was listening to the band back at Fort Ruger Park, near Diamondhead, where they have this big party after the race and Edison comes walking up to me. I was wearing the teal tee shirt with musical instruments from the Honolulu Symphony Fun Run... with tympani's... right about here... (her hands showing they were right around her chest area) and Edison says, 'Nice tympanis'."

I said, "So, that's your best pick up line? Gimme a break." He then said, 'Well then, how about a banana?' I said, "What the hell do I need a banana for?" And then he said, 'I thought you might not know that diaphoresis fluid may have higher concentrations of potassium than you think, but in any case, I wanted to apologize for the unfortunate episode earlier and thought I'd bring you a banana... loaded with potassium you know... and here's an article on the eccrine sweat gland you might find interesting.'

I asked, "You're the gorilla?"

"Yeah..." He said and stuck his hand out to shake.

"And I said something like '... and I thought you were only a big ape.' I mean, how could you not fall for a guy who gives you a banana and an article on the eccrine sweat gland."

"So, Edison, what the hell were you doing in Hawaii?"

"Oh, well... I was actually there alone... on my honeymoon."

"Excuse me?!?" Mel responded.

"My fiancé ran off with her boss three weeks before the wedding... the trip was already paid for... so I said screw it... and thought it would be therapeutic... and... I had an empty seat next to me on the plane... like being in first class... almost"

"Wait a second, here", demanded Mel, "you said you were there on a buying trip for a shipment of ukuleles… and since when were you engaged before… you never told me?!?"

"Uhhhh, well I didn't want to sound like a loser."

Dave, always the one without inhibition inquired,

"Soo…when are you guys getting married?.

Melissa quickly snapped back ,

"I want nothing to do with marriage. My parents went through an ugly divorce and I'm not going to worry about a fuck'in piece of paper that in the end, means absolutely nothing."

Dave, having been put in his place, walked away mumbling something about putting the "shotgun" away for another time.

Julie, in a timely gesture to diffuse the situation, grabbed Melissa's arm and started talking to her about the plan to have an ultra sound done.   Julie, Melissa and Kate began debating the pro's and con's of having the procedure done at this late date.

Kate said, "Melissa you're in your thirties, in the hands of a qualified technician, the procedure should be totally low risk."

"I'm sure everything is OK." Melissa quietly assured, "But I'm still not convinced the sound waves are totally benign to the baby."

"Doctors are the worst patients." Edison observed. "It's like you're sticking your head into the sand."

"Alright already… I'll do it." Melissa relented.

They agreed to make an appointment the next morning.

CHAPTER 10

It's Magical

There were a few moments which developed into a bit of a lull while everyone filled up their plates with food, so Melissa jumped in and announced, "OK, everyone, time for the birthday boy to open his presents!"

It was now time to open some birthday gifts. Edison was apprehensive as not being one to easily accept gifts from people, other than family members. His apprehension was short lived.

The first gift was a cloth baby towel with "World's Cleanest Dad." written on it for feeding time. Everyone dutifully laughed and suggested it be used for midnight feedings, which led to the second gift, a box of gag toothpicks designed to keep one's eyes propped open from staying up all night caring for a baby. After a few more gifts of similar tongue in cheek reminders of first time fatherhood, the last gift was from Kate, a hat with two places for bottles on top, one for baby formula with a nipple on the end and the other for a beer, both to keep father and child mellow.

At that point, the moment Edison feared was beginning to develop.

Will announced, "OK everybody, Edison has received some truly heartwarming gifts, so now it's time for him to give something back. Few of you may know that Edison is a master magician."

Edison loudly cleared his voice wanting to immediately lower the crowd's expectations.

"OK… Edison is a ponderous prestidigitator."

"Get real." Edison replied.

"OK… Edison is slick with the sleight of hand."

Edison shot him another look.

"Alright, alright, Edison knows a couple cool tricks... OK?"

Edison was relieved as he thought Will would pressure him into doing some musical performance, but magic, sure, why not.

Edison had perfected a variety of truly impressive street type maneuvers over the years, using sleight of hand. Fortunately, he always had the ropes, cards and balls in the kitchen utility drawer, and the hidden envelopes and other props already strategically placed around the condo for just such an emergency.

Edison got energized and began with the old standby of tearing up a napkin and making it whole again. Everyone in the room had seen this many times but never grew tired of it and could never quite figure out how he did it. They pestered him time and time again for the secret, but the old magician's credo, do it once and move on… and never reveal the secret prevailed. Always leave them wanting more.

Edison always enjoyed doing magic. He could 'roll' a quarter over his knuckles, manipulate a deck of cards with the best of them and employ sleight of hand along with a good performance to entertain a small group with a good sense of humor. He continued with the cutting of the rope and making it whole again and the mental illusions by getting Dave to name a card already sealed in an envelope tucked under the cushion on the sofa.

His finale was the traditional and ever popular losing his keys, wallet and inhibitions and through effective misdirection and sleight of hand he was able to transform all those objects into one of his favorite snacks, Ritz crackers dipped in applesauce, which tasted surprisingly like apple pie. When he was through, everyone applauded and looked at each other with amusement and delight, even though they all thought he had a very strange choice of snack. Yet, it was this down to earth humor and charm that Melissa found engaging and Kate found natural. Will had participated with Edison as his straight man during the old school days, when they would do some birthdays, bar mitzvahs and anniversaries to scrape together some food money during their Ph.D. days at Mass State.

CHAPTER ELEVEN

Mom

While everyone went back to their small groups, Edison slipped out to the den for a bit of peace and quiet. He turned on his small amplifier very low and picked up his black and white Fender Stratocaster and began playing a few chord progressions. Suddenly the phone rang and the voice-activated caller ID box in the room announced… "Mom".

Edison picked up the phone and his mother was quick to offer up a "Happy Birthday, son. Where have you been all night?"

Edison was very independent and at times like this, he had to remind himself that mom's just being a mother. At that instance, he wondered how he might act the same way, once he is a father. Could it be that he could actually turn into a controlling and meddling helicopter parent like his mother growing up?

He dismissed the possibility. "If I am thinking about it and aware of it, it won't happen." He thought. "I caught it in time."

[MEANWHILE]

In the same dimly lit room as before, the same 19 inch flat LCD screen computer monitor beeped three times. The operator was away getting a cup of coffee and scurried back to the monitor and clicked the mouse to expand to full screen the box titled:

VERIZON ID SYSTEM

Number of origination: 413-555-4893

Dorothy C. Barr
213 Oakridge Dr
Springfield, MA 01110

Number of Target: 413-555-1066

Edison A. Barr
59 Chestnut St
Springfield, MA 01101

Duration of Call: 0:01.3 (increasing in minutes and seconds as time passed)

The operator again pulled up some notes and crosschecked in two different notebooks and nodded, mumbling "You've gotta love this new technology!"

*   *   *

"Have you talked about getting married to Melissa before the baby is born, like I asked you to?" she inquired.
    Edison sighed and retorted,

"Mom, Mel and I will do whatever WE feel is appropriate. I appreciate your interest and I know you care, but we have to do things our way."

"Edison, you're as stubborn as your father. You just don't know what can happen and being married will make sure your child will be protected."

The reference to his father triggered a modestly angry response.

"Mom, what are you talking about? You always say I'm stubborn like Dad when we don't agree with each other, yet you never really tell me anything about him. I've had it with this crap, you make a comment and never explain, why is that?"

"Do you remember the Home Run Derby, when you were just a boy? How stubborn you and Will were, how both of you wouldn't even let one of the fathers pitch to you so you could hit the ball? I just don't want you wasting your life away. You should be doing all that science research stuff you spent 10 years of your life studying in school and not that music... thinking you're going to be some rock star or something. Besides, I want my grandchild to grow up to be a responsible doctor, a surgeon, yeah... a surgeon, helping people get better."

At this point, Edison was on the verge of losing his cool.

"Mom, I'm fed up with all this. I'm a grown man... so after all these years, why won't you tell me about Dad? You always do this to me. You bring up all these comparisons and then shut me off without so much as a hint as to what the hell's going on here. Was he some type of mass murderer or did he commit treason? Is he really dead or is he locked up for life in some jail cell? Damn it, why won't you tell me? For crying out loud, I'm almost forty years old and you still treat me like a child. Listen, I don't want to deal with this now, I'll talk to you on Sunday."

After some heavy breathing on the phone, she responded quietly and half crying,

"You don't know. You just don't know."

Edison just curtly stated,

"Fine. Thanks a lot... and I'll never know until you start trusting me, bye." Edison hung up the phone abruptly and took several deep breaths to regain his composure.

These exchanges ripped his soul apart. His mother was a wonderful mother, yet she would just not talk with him about his own father. He burned inside every time she avoided sharing information about him. She would talk to him about anything else, but not this, the most important stuff he wanted and needed to know about his father, his heritage, his own flesh and blood. Like Will, Edison never knew his father. All his mother ever told him was that he died at work and that a fire, years later destroyed all the family memorabilia, pictures, photographs and everything else about him. He didn't completely believe her. Edison always figured his father was some heinous criminal that would bring shame upon him, maybe even he was still alive and rotting in jail somewhere serving a consecutive triple life sentence without the possibility of parole.

During his days in high school, he spent hours and hours looking up criminal history, trying to find a clue as to what his father must of done. Edison was never able to find anything that would link him with a Dillinger or a Capone or even a Rosenberg. Edison always felt he would rather know what his father must have done, so that he could process it and deal with it and get over it. His mother refused to cooperate. She just patently refused to provide him with the slightest clue as to his heritage.

This void carried through to his other relationships, especially Melissa. Edison was so profoundly disconnected to his past, he couldn't bring himself to share his own history with her, or anyone else, but for Will. Not knowing just ate away at Edison like a cancer, and with the impending birth of his child, the burning was about to become an emotional conflagration.

[MEANWHILE]

Sitting outside Dorothy's house in the Sixteen Acres section of Springfield was a rusting old blue Cadillac. Inside was an older, graying and balding man set in a huge chiseled frame, sculptured jaw and a craggy face with a stare that could send shivers down the faces on Mount Rushmore. A cloud of cigar smoke filled the interior of the Deville and the man was mumbling under his breath. When Dorothy finished her call with Edison and turned out the light next to the phone, the car slowly drove away... with a trail of noticeable bluish gray smoke coming out of the limp exhaust pipe.

* * *

Edison could hear the party breaking up, so he went out to thank everyone and say goodbye. Kate had already pretty much cleaned up and Melissa decided to finish up in the morning and went off to the bedroom. Kate put her hand on Edison's shoulder and gave him a slight squeeze and wished him a happy birthday. Edison thanked her for everything as Kate's hand slowly slid off his shoulder and somehow awkwardly avoided even a platonic hug, as she went for the door. Edison locked the front door and then retreated back into the den, where he went to the closet and dug deep into a box of material and pulled out some framed certificates.

It was a quiet and reflective time for Edison, especially needed on his birthday and the phone conversation with his well meaning but frustrating mother. He needed to be alone for awhile, even though he knew Mel was getting pissed off waiting for him in the bedroom.

The framed certificates were his diplomas, a Bachelor's Degree in Science from Yale and a Master's Degree in Science (Microbiology) from the Massachusetts State University.

He browsed through the Commencement booklet from the Massachusetts State University and found his name listed under the Doctor of Philosophy section.

Edison A. Barr

B.S.   Eli University, Magna Cum Laude
M.S.   The Massachusetts State University
        Microbiology
Major: Biogenetics
        Thesis: Mapping Uncharted Areas of Human
        DNA: A Repository of Ancestral Experience
        (Supervised by Professor J. Reynolds)

He then stared at his doctoral dissertation sitting at the bottom of the box. It was stamped on the cover page "APPROVED" along with a written note, "Pending acceptance by candidate to condition required by J. Reynolds, Advisor."

These were the results of a decade of education, years of research and near world-wide success and fame as a genetic scientist... probing the unmapped nucleotide DNA bands for clues into human heritage. Edison had actually developed a synthesized chemical compound, which would hopefully unlock the existence and function of the heretofore undiscovered intricate layered strands of human DNA.

Edison's Ph.D. dissertation hypothesized that various regions of human DNA contained the chemical imprinted recordation of all the emotional and other experiences of one's ancestors... similar to a laser burning both audio and visual information on a DVD... and that all that was needed was an electro or chemical catalyst to bring that emotional imprint to one's consciousness, and that the child would inherit this recording from both his parents, up to the point of conception. He further hypothesized that actual visual and audio imprints might also exist and recommended further research, as most Ph.D. dissertations conclude.

His research indicated that the most recent generation were delicately wrapped on the outer regions of the strands and the furthest generations were deeply embedded in the core of the respective DNA strand, quite similar to the aging rings on the trunk of a tree. Edison had completed his DNA research faster than 95% of previous Ph.D. candidates and completed all his degree requirements in a phenomenal 3 years. He was offered a huge grant and a prestigious position at one of the best research facilities or a huge salary at the emerging Bio-tech firms popping up around Cambridge and Boston.

Edison's career took a 90 degree turn when he turned down each and every research opportunity. None of the labs would allow him to further synthesize and test his chemical compound without preliminary FDA approval. Edison knew that the politics and bureaucracy would never permit such research on human subjects without decades of double blind studies, mountains of paperwork and zillions of dollars for politics. These studies would just not work on any animal... it had to initiate with human testing.

The underlying principle of his research was that every human being had a genetic imprint upon conception, which could not be altered, but would be harder to access as time passes. The prevailing thought at the time was that a person was partially developed by his or her genetic background and partially by one's environmental inputs. Edison was on the verge of suggesting that a quantum leap needed to be made from traditional Darwinian evolution. The societal and political repercussions of his research were, to put it euphemistically, incendiary. Accusations of genocide, racial and medical suppression would be slung world-wide. If a child was genetically predisposed to a disease, which would cause a likelihood of early death or disability... prohibit that child from educational and other economic and social opportunities while growing up?

The questions were endless, the answers were years, decades and even generations away. In the nineteenth century, it took nearly thirty years for Darwin's theory of evolution and natural selection to gain general acceptance. It took many more decades for society to catch up with the science. And there are those even today that refute the science. Here, all bets were off. If the Scopes case was the trial of the century, then surely, somewhere a trial would ensue and be the modern day trial equivalent of the holocaust. It would be the trial of the coming new millennium. Something inside of Edison convinced him to opt out of the life-long certainty of conflict and the probable non-resolution of this conundrum during his lifetime.

The clincher was the conflict with the FDA. Without its approval for testing, Edison's research had nowhere to go. No legitimate research facility would allow him to pursue his true passion. Certainly, he would be compromised by economic factors to engage with a more commercially viable field of study. At that point, Edison made a pilgrimage to Skinner Park atop Holyoke mountain in South Hadley, a place where Edison always went to think through all of his critical life decisions. Skinner Park was Edison's sanctuary. The view from atop the mountain was to put it mildly, spectacular. One could see on a clear day, miles away with some of the most interesting natural vistas available in all New England, the Ox Bow of the Connecticut River, downtown Northampton, LaFleur Airport, the University of Massachusetts and all the way down to Springfield and Hartford.

After several hours pondering his future and options at that time, Edison stood up at the edge of the mountain side and proclaimed at dusk at the top of his voice,

"I need more music!"

CHAPTER 12

The Torch has been Passed to a New Generation

The mood was a bit somber in the squad room this morning. News had just come that Ernie Dugan, veteran detective on the force for 40 years before retiring had passed away the night before. The squad room was quite different than when Ernie started out as a rookie detective. Back then there were large wooden desks, heavy chairs, large wooden file cabinets, large round desk lamps, creaky wooden floors. Now, the room was full of metal desks with swivel fabric backed chairs with lumbar support, bright modern colors, push button telephones, computer screens on every desk and the ultimate, air conditioning. One by one each detective and uniformed cop came by to Tom's desk to offer his or her condolences.

Tom had recently made detective on the same police force as his father. Ernie had a profound impact on Tom's choice of career. It's certainly not that Ernie pressured him. Tom's mother, Nancy, would not have approved of that. She worried every day when the phone rang, if it would be the call informing her that Ernie was shot and killed. She didn't want that for Tom. Tom's fate was more than likely sealed years ago, an integral part of his DNA.

It was in his blood. Tom used to hang on every word...
every move of Ernie. Tom saw it like a chess game, planning
one move after another, positioning, trading, and ultimately,
gaining checkmate on the crooks. Tom innately understood
that 90% of his effort would be homework and legwork.

The funeral was well attended by all of the available
officers and detectives. The mayor and all the city
councilmen made an appearance. The procession had so
many cars, it looked like it would stretch across town. It was
a cool morning and black was the color of the day. Ernie's
widow, Nancy never thought it would end this way, a heart
attack complicated by a stroke. Tom and his younger sister
were attending their mother, one on each arm, almost holding
her up.

One by one, the mourners filed by the casket, offering
their condolences to the family. Tom could hear some of the
older detectives snicker under their breaths that Ernie
probably had the heart attack and stroke as a result of never
giving up on 'The Case'. Comments like "I told you he'd go
to his grave before solving that case." were heard more than
once. Tom knew the frustration experienced by his father,
the indignity of not being able to solve the very first case
assigned to him as a detective, over a forty year career.

As the last of the mourners filed past, the family had a
last moment with the casket.

Finally, Tom was alone with his father for a final
promise. Tom whispered "Dad, no matter what, no matter
how long it takes, no matter how much money, no matter
what... I'll solve the case, I promise you. Don't give up, I'll
do it. We'll do it, Pop."

Chapter 13

And the Band Played On

Big Notes was especially busy today, everyone preparing for the annual 'Road to Fame' concert this Friday, where many local talents would gear up for the once in a lifetime opportunity to impress a local or regional independent recording company talent agent. Every year during the Western Mass Arts Festival, Edison opened up the doors, constructed a temporary stage along the sidewalk at the intersection, with a red and white striped awning so that anyone who felt that they were just a step away from a music recording career could throw caution to the wind and give it a shot.

For the most part, there would be a dozen or so vocalists, musicians or groups ranging from the standards, folk music, rapping, classical guitar or just some good old pop or rock 'n roll. Usually, the open mike nights at the Iron Horse Café in Northampton would be the magnet for these types, but during the summer, the outdoor opportunity would allow the wannabe talents to pretend to be playing in Fenway Park, writ small. Generally, some the would-be talent bordered on passable bar or coffee house entertainment, while most wouldn't even make it to the finals of a local bar's karaoke night.

A couple acts were always near embarrassing and yet somehow, each year there were always one or two that were a pleasant surprise, enough so that a couple of reps from private recording studios would always attend the event. They would offer some studio time to see if something might come of it. At worst, the music attracted attention enough to engage others attending the other arts and craft displays and Edison's business would also peak a bit during the festival. Besides, the Museum Arts Council, which sponsored the Festival, always appreciated Edison's attempts to bring in a crowd and help create a critical mass for a promising annual downtown event.

Edison always offered a nice prize to the act, which generated the biggest audience and the largest applause. This year he had a brand new Roland keyboard with MIDI and other attachments, so he expected a nice turnout. Kevin and Mike were college students at Western New England College up in the Sixteen Acres section of Springfield and had a group of their own, but Edison wouldn't let them play at the Festival, kind of like the promotions where employees and their families were not eligible and void in Minnesota and Wisconsin or some other nonsense. Edison didn't want to get into any kind of legal hassles. They were wiring amps and speakers together with microphones and generally handling some customers.

Kate walked in and found Edison in the repair area intensely concentrating of a mass of wires and alligator clips and little boxes all wired together in a convoluted, yet arguably artistic configuration. There were volt meters, oscilloscopes showing wave shapes and a computer recording various tones in digital format. She was carrying a balky bag of items along with her handbag and a white paper bag, which looked like her lunch.

"You look like you need a break…"

"Today... at McDonald's" Edison chimed in without so much as losing a beat, mimicking the memorable ad jingle, looking at her lunch.

Kate responded a bit defensive, "Well, sometimes you just gotta have some junk food with french fries. Know what I mean... want some?"

"Tempting, but not right now." Edison played back. He decided he did need a short break after all and wiped his brow realizing he could use some time away from his project. "I've got to tweak this just a bit for an important client." he innocently observed, without any pretentious intent whatsoever.

Kate knew this but wanted to pull his chain a bit, so she queried, "Oh, like the Stones?"

Edison, still preoccupied with his project merely responded honestly and matter of fact, "Nah, he was here last month, won't be seeing those guys for awhile... on tour in Europe anyway."

 Kate thought he was playing his deadpanned humor to the hilt and just laughed it off, not realizing that Edison was telling it to her straight. She enjoyed the banter with Edison and appreciated his dry sense of humor, in stark contrast to Melissa. Although good friends with Melissa, Kate had to do lunch out of the lab, just to get away and wondered how Edison could deal with it all the time.

Kate plopped down her shopping bag and began to show Edison its contents and asked,

"Did you get your scuba stuff yet? Look what I got." She pulled out a pair of black flippers about a foot long with a heel rest on the end, a green, pink and purple BCD (Buoyancy Compensation Device) vest, a diving mask with surgical silicone head band with snorkel attached and a compass.

Edison looked over the equipment and asked,

"Is that everything you need? And before you answer that, how much did it cost?"

"Well," she responded, "the dive guy gives you a package deal if you buy it all together, yes, but you won't need the compass. I on the other hand, have a knack for getting lost." playing with the compass.

Somehow Edison understood her response, despite its non- sequitur.

"Like I said, how much?"

"Well, it depends mostly on what BCD you buy. I got this one, it was kind of middle in the price range." She then held it up to Edison joking, "I think these colors work for you."

"I'll be looking for something with a little more of that Y chromosome look to it, thank you very much."

Kate retorted, "Well, in that case, he had one just like this… except there wasn't any… green!" With that, Kate knew it was time to exit and asked him one more time if he wanted some french fries and if not, she had better be getting back to the lab.

"Don't want to get in trouble with the boss." referring to Melissa.

"I thought she was going to the dive shop with you."

"Oh yeah, she did… and wait 'til you see what she got. She just went to the nail place for a quick touch up."

Kate packed up her things and walked toward the door and with one last parting shot,

"Hey, can I play the flute on Friday? I used to do a pretty mean Sousa Stars and Stripes Forever."

Edison, again not missing a beat retorted,

"Sure, but I can't guarantee I'll be able to hold the crowd back, you know how they attack rock stars. Just make sure your health insurance is paid up."

Edison experienced the ends of his lips curve upward and just as abruptly swiveled around and started attacking his project again.

CHAPTER 14

Lab rats

Kate half dashed back into the lab with about nine seconds left to her lunch hour, still realizing she had to actually eat back at her table. Hopefully Melissa would not be overly sarcastic today. Kate was feeling good now and didn't care for any hassles. Fortunately, she beat Melissa back to the lab. Kate was inhaling her McD's special when Julie and Dave came by her desk.

The lab was not like anything right out of a Boris Karloff movie, but nonetheless, there was no mistaking this place for an ice cream parlor. One corner of the lab contained a half dozen strange looking mazes with all types of contraptions mounted on them. Some were electronic equipment for monitoring things and others were mirrors, lights and Lucite boxes containing various food stuffs. On the other corner was what looked like a full blown chemistry kit. Beakers, test tubes, Bunsen burners, jars of various compounds and vials of liquids and the obligatory periodic table chart covering almost the entire wall. Desks and file cabinets were aligned in one corner and Melissa's office in the other.

Melissa had been hired as the manager of the project last year, after doing a long stint with a similar lab doing experiments in oncology and aging. Melissa was enticed to this project with an offer of managerial control and a one and a half times increase in her salary, which already had plenty of zero's and a comma to it.

Kate, Dave, Hank and Julie were already working on the same team, so Melissa was the new kid on the block for this project. They had a grant from the American Science Foundation that could be milked for at least four years and possibly longer if some tangible results were discovered.

Several bio-tech firms around the Route 128 area of Boston were looking for background data for some Alzheimer genetically re-engineered drugs which had a huge market potential for the oncoming tidal wave of baby boomers entering their fifties. The firms were flush with cash from venture capitalists and funded these special projects through the Foundation for specialized narrow R&D tax benefits.

The group had been running tests on lab rats to determine the acquisition of memory or the loss of it from one generation to another. The basic premise was to teach a sample group of rats the solution to a maze in order to reap the almost Pavlov reward of a hunk of sharp yellow cheddar cheese. Once the sample 'learned' the most direct route through the maze, they were mated and then the progeny were tested to determine if there was any statistical improvement of the second generation. The mated rats were mated in a plethora of combinations and later re-tested against their progeny.

About a couple months ago, the research took a somewhat bizarre turn. As a result of the Belk-Carter research group in California, delivered a paper at the American Research Psychology Association on memory improvements in lab rats from ingested food groups. Dave then developed the neo-Frankenstein type strategy. When the ancestor test rats died, their brains were surgically extracted, ground up and fed to a new set of rats, some genetically connected to the ancestor and others, which were not.

This is where the group is now and the current topic is the most efficient way to get the brain material to the new rats while minimizing the chemical loss to their brains. Right now that meant, intravenous injections or "brain burgers" … fed under normal feeding patterns.

Dave wandered over to Kate's desk while she was finishing the last of her now limp french fries.

"Did you take in what Melissa's husband was talking about the other night?"

"First off, they're not married.." she insisted.

"Oh, I figured, since Melissa's, like .. "

"Yeah… like knocked up?"

"No… well OK, yeah, you know what I mean."

"Well, you mean that comment about..."

"Taking the wrong approach. Accessing the ancestral DNA?"

"Yeah, what's your take on that?"

"The more I find out about Edison, I don't think much gets passed him."

"Well, it's been bugging me ever since. You know how my mind works."

"Yeah, I know. You're the one who came up with the "brain cheeseburgers.""

"Exactly. Anyway, I decided to do a search in EBISCO and SearchBank, (academic electronic data bases for publications and dissertations) and guess what I came up with?"

"Gallbladder burgers?"

"Seriously."

"Gallbladder burgers wouldn't be serious?"

"Forget the burgers! Look at this."

SEARCH RESULTS:

Title: Mapping Uncharted areas of Human DNA: A Repository of Ancestral Experiences.

Subject: Genetics, DNA, Molecular Biology

Source: Mass State University, Pattee Library

Author: Edison A. Barr

Abstract: Focuses on identifying and mapping of sections of human DNA. The hypothesis and accompanying recommended exploration and testing procedures encompass unmapped sections of the nucleotide bands which contain the possible recordation of collective prior life experiences of one's ancestors, layered in nucleotide strands from the most recent on the exterior, to the most distant at the core.

AN: 99900001112345
ISSN: 1066-12345
Note: D'Amour Library doesn't
              have this title.

RESULT LIST: PRINT / E-MAIL / SAVE

Kate gazed intently over the print out. Her eyes were focusing in and out, digesting the impact of the document. She was intermittently shocked, amused, impressed, overwhelmed and speechless. If there was any doubt about her progressing feelings for Edison, all doubt was now erased. Curiously, at this moment, all she could think about was how she knew she had a major problem on her hands, which is why all she could say was in a controlled and understated expression.

"Wow."

"I know we were all laughing at him under our breaths, but there was just something that rang true, and this certainly is a ball buster." "Why hasn't Melissa told us about him.?" Dave asked.

Just as he was finishing that thought, Melissa returned from her nail visit and inquired,

"Tell you about what?"

"About Edison." Dave asserted sort of matter of fact.

"What about Edison?"

"About his genetic research?"

"Are you nuts. The only thing Edison knows about genes is deciding whether to buy Levi's or Wrangler's."

Both Dave and Kate were genuinely shocked at the response. Kate, after the initial reaction, developed a smile, which she was fighting to hold back. She knew it couldn't be all that great with Edison and Melissa if this huge of a schism existed between them, and that meant she actually had a chance, at least in her imagination. The meat hook had sunk in. She was powerless. Kate's thoughts were running rampant, faster than the backstretch at the Kentucky Derby. "She's pregnant with his baby." "My job." "Melissa's a good friend, a boss." "Oh, god, this is worse than a soap opera love triangle... and I'm the one stuck with the unrequited love."

Her thoughts were interrupted abruptly when the moment of cold silence was shattered by Melissa's reaction. Dave had dropped the abstract in Melissa's hands. Each of them was uneasy for totally different reasons. Dave and Kate delicately awaited some tangible response. It was not long in coming. Denial.

"This has to be another Edison A. Barr." "This can't be…" She huffed.

But in her heart she knew it was her Edison. She knew that Will and Edison had been to Mass State together and realized there might be another Edison A. Barr somewhere else, but not there. She also immediately synthesized all of the off the cuff comments Edison had made to her in the gorilla suit all the way to the party and the lab team… that it all now made sense. It was like a picture puzzle with missing pieces. This puzzle took on a whole new life with the addition of the last pieces creating the whole picture.

She then knew that there were things, important things about Edison that she knew nothing about. She always knew they might not have the greatest relationship in the world, but that it was strong enough to work out. He was so thrilled about the baby.

It's not that finding out that your baby's father wrote an esoteric Ph.D. dissertation is such a heinous discovery, but such a major component of his life, intentionally kept from her. "Why?" she thought. "My god", she continued to herself, "he's probably more qualified to run this project than I am."

The hook that at the same instance had just settled into Kate's psyche, had just been ripped out of Melissa's. Newton's Third Law… once again applied to everyday life. Her immediate thought on the subject was "How dare he do this to me?"

Julie felt very uncomfortable in this awkward situation and felt it necessary to change the topic and asked Melissa, "I know you want all of us to take two weeks of vacation time after you give birth, so do you have any update on when then might be... airline tickets need to be purchased at least a couple weeks ahead of time to save some money?"

"Plan on next week. If this load doesn't drop by next Wednesday, I'm going to insist on a C-section on Thursday."

CHAPTER 15

Oh what a tangled World Wide Web

Will's call to Edison sounded a bit panicky. That's why Edison agreed to go over to Will's office. Edison didn't have much time to spare at the store, but Will wasn't prone to emotionalism. That's what Edison valued in their friendship. Edison was a bright individual with an eclectic love for life, tempered by the insulation from his past, which he lived with on a daily basis. When Edison would feel detached, Will was always there to provide an anchor, at least to his known past, the tangible benefit of being childhood pals. Will was the only one who could relate.

Edison walked in Will's office, a place he hadn't been to for years. For some reason, they always met at Big Notes, or on the tennis court. It was after hours and the rest of the offices were dark and the glow out from the office reminded Edison of the scene from E.T. in the shed. Since Edison was always trying to maintain his grip for tennis, he generally had a tennis ball he squeezed, in his coat pocket. Edison tossed the ball into the office, startling Will. Edison waited a moment to see if the ball would be coming back at him, but it didn't. Will wasn't on the same wavelength today. Nonetheless, without appreciating the humor of the moment, Will knew it was Edison.

"Come on in Eddy boy. I assume you're your shagging a tennis ball you just hit out from Forest Park." (the local tennis courts, several miles away). "Was it an errant serve or just a bad return of service?"

Edison was immediately deluged with post-it notes, tacked onto just about every possible free inch of space. Some were pink, some were blue, some were white, but mostly, those ubiquitous yellow squares, plastered everywhere. Edison immediately wondered how such an accomplished and organized computer specialist could manage those notes all over the place. It was like a C.P.A. who couldn't balance his own checkbook. Shortly, Edison was to find out the scattered post-it notes were just the logical extension of Will's random-access thought processes.

"Hey, Will, what's up?" "You sounded a bit nervous on the phone." Edison offered up.

"Sit down." Was the direct response. As Edison started to sit at the opposing side of his desk, Will hastened to add, "No, over here so you can see the computer screen."

Will, being at the vanguard of his profession, naturally had a flat screen LCD 20" NEC monitor, which was less than 1" wide. Since the viewing angle was a bit restricted, apparently, Will wanted Edison to share what was on the screen directly.

Will asked Edison, already knowing the answer, "Do you know that much about the Internet?"

"I know the Web is divided into three parts." "I browse, I click, I download." "Et tu"? Edison showing off his love for Latin, trying to lighten the moment a bit.

"Thanks." "Did you just have a Caesar salad at Bertucci's or something?" Will rallied back. "You asked me to check out the mortgages for that Longmeadow house, remember?"

The word "remember" turned Edison a bit sarcastic,

"I know I'm at the forty barrier, but I haven't been diagnosed with Alzheimer's as yet, or have I?" Edison didn't realize that Will was just setting him up for an overhead smash.

"Well, I did and wait 'til you see what I found."

Edison immediately thought,

"You called me over here in a hurry because you found a mortgage rate ¼ pt below the prevailing rate?" But the conversation was about to turn towards dessert.

"Have you ever heard of a cookie?" "And no chocolate chip or Oreo jokes."

"Well, in that case, no." Edison felt deprived of the last shot of banter.

"A cookie is a generally a small file sent back from a Web site back to the inquiring computer, and embedded in a subdirectory file in your computer." Will started. "You can never be sure, but they're supposed to be rather benign. Unless you're aware of it, you probably have hundreds of cookies sent back to you through the Web that are residing in your hard drive. As soon as we're through here, I want to go back to your place and take an inventory of the cookies in your computer at home. But for now, the other side of cookies are traces or tags left by other inquiring computers that are "residue" on various internet sites. These traces can be picked up if too much time hasn't passed since the hit took place. Are you keeping up with this?"

Edison, always interested in learning, said,

"Strangely, yes, at least so far."

"Well, pal, you've been tagged."

"Say what?"

When you gave me your social security number, I checked to see if there would be any credit problems, like sort of doing an unofficial credit check on you."

"Are you saying I've got a credit problem?" "No way! I must get an unsolicited credit card letter every other day."

"It's not that you have a credit problem. It's that you have a credit PROBLEM." You've been tagged. That means that someone has been checking up on you, and I don't mean just a little."

Will pulled a post-it note from the corner of the monitor.

"Here, someone has been checking into your credit history." He then started pulling post-it notes from all over the room, one by one showing he was indeed organized, just not in a traditional file cabinet format. "Here, someone has been checking on your safe deposit boxes. Here, someone has been checking on your auto registration. Here, someone has been checking on your driving record. Here, someone has been checking on your bank accounts. Here, someone has been checking on your marital status. Here, someone has been checking on your phone records. Here, someone has been checking on your credit card purchases. Here, someone has been checking on your food purchases. Here..."

Edison interrupted,

"I'm getting the message. Couldn't this all be normal. I did file a pre-mortgage application with BancBoston awhile ago."

Will assured him,

"No way, Jose. The coding, the addresses are all the same, not a bank, either. These addresses are from some official agency. Not the FBI or CIA or anything, because they would've erased their inquiries, but it looks like some governmental agency, though, like a police department, who doesn't know better to erase their snooping. Are you having any trouble with the IRS. It could be them, if you haven't filed tax returns."

"Are you kidding, I just filed a few months ago. I was audited about two-three years ago and ended up getting money back from them because I didn't claim a deduction I was entitled to. They told me I couldn't be audited for several years."

"Well, then, you haven't applied for some secret job or security clearance behind my back, have you?"

"Yeah, I want to work for the FBI, so that I can be assigned to the 'X' file project." Edison confessed, feeling the need for sarcasm.

"Well, then, I'll have to check your computer to get any more information on this. The signature tags that I've found from here aren't, … I can't seem to identify them, but they seem to be local." Will continued to punch some keys and do some clicks on the mouse.

Edison's insecurity about his past immediately crept into his mind.

"My father must've been convicted of something horrible and did time at Alcatraz. Now they're-checking up on me. Crap, I don't even know if we have the same last name. How could there be any confusion? He must be out of prison and doing something illegal again. Damn it mother. This has got to end. I'm not going to take no for an answer. I'll get her over for dinner and won't let her go until I get some answers."

A stray thought also entered his mind. His Ph.D. dissertation. (Edison always planned alternative means to the ends.)

CHAPTER 16

Ultra Sound Wave

Melissa was unusually uneasy this morning. Generally, she is always in control, focused, calculating and directed. Edison wrote it off to the uncertainty of the ultrasound which she was to undergo today. Even though they had thoroughly discussed the pros and cons of the procedure, she was uncomfortable with the decision, blaming her tentativeness on the sound wave impact on the baby, when in fact she was apprehensive seeing an almost fully developed baby was getting too close to reality. Edison guessed that when push came to shove, some apprehension is to be expected, unaware of her actual concerns. Edison appreciated this uncertain side of Melissa, a nice contrast from her usual self-assured somewhat aggressive personality.

Melissa had not confronted Edison with the discovery of his Ph.D. dissertation on genetics. She wanted to wait for the right moment, a dinner at a restaurant, so he couldn't do anything unexpected. Better yet, maybe having his mother over for dinner would be the appropriate time. With the both of them there, maybe she'd get to the whole truth out of one of them. Edison had asked her last night if it would be OK to have his mother over for dinner. Perfect. She thought to herself, "But how Will I initiate this." The uncertainty was making her uneasy.

This was probably fine, since she actually began worrying about the procedure, since the baby was moving now with rapid movement. She knew that the unexpected movement could be a problem and a successful picture would be difficult and she still wasn't 100% convinced of the safety of the ultra sound waves on the fetus.

Dr. Blackman's office on Maple Street was a typical neo-fifties medical office, replete with medical/industrial wallpaper, with a mind numbing nautical pattern, thin wooden chairs with the obligatory three or four shades of vinyl, a reception area with the sliding glass with the traditional Norman Rockwell scene right out of Leave it to Beaver.

Edison confirmed the appointment through the sliding glass and started wondering how the visit would go. He was keenly aware of Melissa's aggressive personality and what horrible patients doctors make with other doctors. He was afraid it would be like …

They filled out the standard insurance forms and began to peruse the choice of magazines available. Months old issues of Sports Illustrated, Reader's Digest or Parent. They waited for about 15 minutes. Curiously, nothing was exchanged between the two of them. Just idle glances at the other couples in the waiting room.

Fortunately, Dr. Blackman, a man of fifty something was cool, confident and self-assured while still having a quiet and friendly demeanor. After only thirty seconds, Edison knew that his concerns would be unfounded. Perhaps, because he knew that Melissa was an M.D., he immediately took control without being offensive.

"I'm glad you decided to have this done. I'm sure you'll both feel comfortable knowing exactly where things stand. Now let's see, you were referred by Dr. Frederick – good man, in fact my wife uses him. Everything OK on that end?"

"Dr. Frederick came highly recommended and he's been wonderful." Melissa offered. "I trust him implicitly. He said you have good procedural technique, which is why we're here."

Edison wasn't sure if she was trying to win him over with a compliment or setting the bar high enough to motivate him to do his best work. Fortunately, he took it as a compliment.

"I guess that five bucks I bribed him with paid off." he quipped.

Edison's comfort with the situation was about to evaporate.

"Well, before we go into the examination room with the sonogram, let's get some background material on both of you."

Edison had failed to anticipate the questions about familial history and now realized that it was about to hit the fan, as he put his hands on both sides of his head and tentatively pulled on his hair as if to clear his mind.

"Ed, may I call you Ed?" Dr. Blackman started, wanting to dissipate any anxiety he perceived Edison may have had.

"Sure, as long as you don't put a Mr. in front of it." Ed instinctively responded, a line he has had to use innumerable times in his life.

Dr. Blackman showed his control of the situation by deadpanning,

"Don't worry, I won't horse around."

"Ed, are your parents still alive?"

"My mother is, but my father is dead." Edison provided. This killed Edison inside. Whenever asked, that was his pat response, although in his heart, he has steadfastly believed that his father was still alive lingering in some jail cell, and that his mother told him he was dead to bring finality to his incessant questioning as a child. Edison certainly knew the importance of the question and the subsequent questions. The genetic background would provide a foundation for by suggesting various ancillary tests. Edison was wrenching inside because he could only give half an answer. Edison was thorough, careful and thoughtful in everything he did. All Edison could think of was to get his mother backed into a corner and badger her until she finally relented. Dr. Blackman snapped Edison out of his train of thought.

"Are you aware of any genetic problems in either your mother's or father's families?"

"None that I'm aware of in my mother's family and I really don't know about my father, he died when I was an infant and my mother hasn't told me much about him... medically speaking." he apologized.

Out of nowhere, Melissa chimed in under her breath, "Oh, I see. Apparently it must be hereditary."

Edison shot back an incredulous look, while Dr. Blackman looked like, "Here we go again."

Edison gave Melissa a look,

"We'll talk about this later," and continued, "... but I don't believe there are any problems, to my knowledge."

Edison could only think of his mother, until he saw the outline of his child through the sonogram. Dr. Blackman then asked,

"Do you want to know the sex of the baby?" "Because if you don't, close your eyes right now."

Edison slowly but firmly developed one of the biggest smiles ever seen on an expectant father's face, implicitly recognizing that the mere asking the question provided the answer. The baby's sex was evident to even the untrained eye. Just at that moment, the baby was moving its arm as if to be waving at them. They all had a good laugh and the rest of the appointment went without incident. They left the office knowing that the lab results would be available later in a couple days.

CHAPTER 17

Cocktail Hour

Edison and Will ended up a local Danny's after their monthly poker game, which is the only place open all late and serves breakfast at any time. Edison felt like a light breakfast, since was still hungry after the game. He always felt the urge to eat when something heavy was going on. Will knew this from their Mass State days, where they would spend hours eating and re-eating the next meal at the New College Diner. Despite their different graduate areas of study, they always appreciated each other to bounce ideas and problems off the other. They each respected the other for his objectivity and general intelligent approach to problem solving.

They hadn't done this type of meeting for a year or so and the mood was decidedly retro, but for the lack of a New College Diner in Springfield. Will was stoked to get into the cookie and WWW situations and Edison was going to solicit Will's help for an even more bizarre adventure, in order to get to the bottom of his father's history.

As they sat down, a family of four was sitting in the booth next to them and a server named 'Scott' was taking their order. Upon completing that order, he moved over to their table and asked if there was anything he could get them to start. They both ordered iced tea and began to review the menu.

"I might have to call in some outside expertise to identify the tags and cookies all over your reports." Will opened. "Do you have any objection, if I make sure of their total ability to maintain your privacy?"

"Uh, yeah." Edison responded half-heartedly.

Will picked up on this and immediately they were in their old established mode of operation, as if no time had passed since the last time. Generally, one of them had a pressing problem and the other upon finding out what it was would yield to the other. After some resolution of that first matter, they would order again and attack the other's problem. This time, the focus was on Edison for both reasons, it was him being tagged by some anonymous government hacker and whatever else that had him preoccupied.

Scott came by with their drinks and they proceeded to order some food. Edison ordered the combination of scrambled eggs with bacon and pancakes, while Will went straight for the waffles with fruit.

"Will, I'm sure you remember my proposed research experiment back at Mass State?" Edison proceeded cautiously.

Of course Will did, it was the trigger that caused Edison to decline his Ph.D. degree at the last minute before graduation.

"And, from what you've heard over the past couple weeks, you know where I'm going with this?" He continued with some hesitation in his voice.

"All I got tonight was the same old stuff. You want to find out about your father and your mother's not …"

"It's that, but more now." Edison interrupted.

"How much more?" Will asked, sort of throwing out the fishing line to see what he might catch.

"All the way." Edison provided with the first hint of conviction in his voice. "I've got to take it all the way.

"You've got to be kidding." Will responded with equal conviction.

They were interrupted by Scott, bringing their meals.

"Let's see, you have the breakfast combo and you have the waffles." he stated, somewhat proud that he got the order right. "Is there anything else you want?"

Before either of them could answer, the father in the booth next to them piped up emphatically,

"Yes there is." He continued, "We ordered way before they did, so why don't we have our meals, yet?"

Scott continued to await a response from Edison and Will, without responding to the black family in the next booth. Edison's interest was re-directed to the people in the next booth and not on his meal. Scott hemmed and hawed but could only muster a weak "Uh, I'm not sure." "Let me check back in the kitchen."

The father was becoming agitated by Scott's indifference. Edison could hear him responding to his wife in muted anger.

"Darling, I don't care." "They just signed a goddamn consent decree with the Justice Department to treat black customers with respect, besides you're the one who insisted things would be better." "I swear, if we don't get served immediately, I'll have someone in the office file a complaint."

Edison still hadn't begun to touch his meal and Will was just pecking at it knowing, based upon numerous past experiences of Edison diligently sticking up for him because of his race...that something was about to happen.

Scott returned and sheepishly informed them, "Uh, like someone back there, like lost your order and, uh, could I like maybe get it again?"

Before the father could even utter a syllable, Edison barked out at Scott, "Listen you moron, the boy had a child's meal, a hot dog and fries with a 7-Up in a kiddie cup, the girl had an order of pancakes, with a side of bacon, crispy please, with a large glass of milk, Mom had the Chef's salad with romaine lettuce instead of iceberg, light Italian dressing on the side and hold the tomatoes with a coffee, cream, no sugar and Dad had bacon cheese burger, extra well done, crisp bacon, Swiss cheese, on a sesame seed bun, please don't toast it, a side order of cole slaw instead of the french fries and an ice tea with lemon!" pause... "And if you don't have it here, like pronto, I'll like..."

Will grabbed his arm and tried to turn him around to their own table, merely imploring,

"Eddy, please." Even though it was Will who should've been annoyed to this level for such a racial situation.

Edison, only at that moment, knew he might have gone just a bit over the line and settled down.

Scott scampered off and the family just sat there stunned and couldn't say a word. They just kept looking at Edison and whispering to themselves, but Edison couldn't see this as he finally turned around and began to eat his eggs.

"At least it's nice to see at least that some things never change." Will commented. "Actually, that was one of your milder outbursts, you must be mellowing with age."

"Nah", said Edison, "It just bugs the hell out of me to see that kind of crap." "I just can't help it. I just don't know how you can stand for that crap."

"Now, you've got to be kidding." Will shifted back to the original conversation.

"About that?"

"No, about your experiment. Listen, I'll be the first to admit I don't really know what in the hell it's all about, but you can't be serious about resurrecting that Frankenstein bullshit. Christ, they were ready to arrest you, a first for the Ph.D. candidate, I might add. Most people were worried about getting arrested by the DEA narc agents and there you were about to be busted by the plain old FDA. Christ, that would've been embarrassing. I'll bet ol' Jay Reynolds is still telling first year candidates about you, to scare the hell out of them. What could possibly be getting you back into that stuff?

"Will, listen, do the calculations. Someone is going out of his way to invade my privacy, playing Big Brother… my mother is telling so many lies about my father, that she can't even keep them straight anymore… I'm about to have a son and I can't even tell the doctor anything about my father's medial history, I have nothing to tell my son when he grows up, and I've been wanting to do this for 15 years now."

After the introduction of the problem, the protocol was to finish the food and prepare for round two. They both instinctively took great pains to surgically dissect and eat their food, in order to allow some time to intervene.

Edison broke the silence…

"Will, nothing's really changed in 15 years." "The experiment is even more valid today than it was back then, given the quantum leap science has taken in mapping DNA with the Genome Project."

Will retorted, "Just like you said, nothing has changed." You're still talking about a drug… synthesized from LSD for crying out loud… my god… what are you thinking? Do you really want to risk frying your brain, especially with a baby on the way? You're not by yourself anymore, you've got responsibilities damn it."

The last comment seemed to penetrate Edison's stubborn focus on finding out about his father.

Just then, the family in the next booth got up to leave. After eating their meal, they weren't in any mood to hang around for dessert. The father walked over to Edison and simply said,

"Thank you."

Edison responded apologetically,

"Uh, I'm sorry." "I uh, hope I didn't cause you any embarrassment. I just..."

"Hey, don't worry, the boy deserved it." Maybe he learned a lesson, besides, may I ask what you do for a living? Assuming you weren't intentionally eavesdropping, I was quite impressed with your memory back there."

"Well, I own the ah, Big Notes music store downtown."

"Aha, well when my children take up an instrument, I'll be sure to look you up. If I can ever repay the favor, let me know." The father said as he handed Edison his business card.

Chester R. Gibbons, III
Robinson, Gibbons, Mayer and Katz
Attorneys at Law
2300 Valley Tower
Springfield, MA 01101
(413) 555-2300

When Will looked at the card, he pointed out,

"You'd better keep this, he's that big time civil rights attorney who's supposed to be running for the Senate next year.

Will and Edison decided to end this particular session and Edison agreed he would not do anything further without Will's input. They got their check from another server, as apparently Scott was not about to show his face again that night. Edison flipped out his MasterCard and told Will it was on him, being his problems this time. Will and Edison would usually fight over the bill, but this time Will relented gave his credit card with the bill.

[MEANWHILE]

The computer screen beeped. The operator was not in front of the screen. The screen saver was in operation, but when the beep occurred the main screen came back on and a notification   scrolled   across   the   screen.

Credit card approval # 1711452
　　Danny's Restaurant # 59820
　　Bicentennial Hwy Springfield, MA

　　Edison A. Barr, cardholder
　　Expiration Date: 10/99
　　Charge: $14.15
　　 06/21/9x 21:38 PM

CHAPTER 18

Big Brother to the Rescue

Edison's mother had settled in for the night, watching CNN. She heard a noise coming from the kitchen. She dismissed it as some pots and pans settling in the cabinet and continued to catch up on the day's news. Watching the news always had a soothing effect. She always preferred knowing what's going on and felt uneasy when she didn't know what was happening.

She lived in a six-room ranch in a subdivision in the sixteen acres section of Springfield. The house was built in the late 50's or early 60's. It is where Edison grew up. The house was a white ranch with clapboard exterior with a one car attached garage. There was a living room with a couch, several chairs, a spinet piano and a coffee table. The furniture had plastic covers and the coffee table had a few books on art and travel and music. There was sheet music on the piano, the Maple Leaf Rag by Scott Joplin. The standing joke was that if she was ever able to master that song, Edison would cut a record for her. So far, there's been no record, although she dutifully plugs away in the afternoons, measure by measure.

There were three bedrooms and one and a half baths. The half bath was off of the master bedroom. She was watching TV in the den, a small bedroom with a reclining chair, a sewing machine and a curio cabinet filled with various trinkets.

The kitchen and dining area were off the living room on the other side of the house with a rear door leading out to the back yard, which still had the worn grass markings of a small baseball diamond from Edison's boyhood.

It was a warm early summer night and she had the windows open to generate a breeze through the house. Fortunately, the prevailing winds provided a nice breeze such that air conditioning was rarely needed. Unfortunately, these prevailing winds blew all of the maple and oak leaves from all of the neighbors' houses onto hers during the Fall. They were so plentiful, that she rarely raked up all of the leaves from the previous fall, before the new batch started building up.

It was when she heard the crunch of leaves that she looked up from the TV and got up out of her chair and peeked out the window in the den to see if anything was out there. Everything looked quiet, so she sat back down and resumed watching TV. It was probably the neighbor's cat.

She felt the urge for a cold drink after watching a commercial and got up and walked down the hallway to the kitchen. The wall plate switch was located in a non-intuitive position, around the corner leading into the kitchen. Even though she lived there for about forty years, she still always went to flip on the light switch were there was none. Tonight was no different. She felt the empty wall and muttered to herself, "How many more years is it going to take me."

As she turned to flick on the actual switch in the dark, she felt an arm and a gloved hand, the size of frying pan grab her from behind and cover her mouth. She was so startled that even without the gloved hand over her mouth she would not have been able to utter a sound, let alone a scream. Her mouth might have frozen up, but her body reacted instinctively and violently squirmed and shook like a convulsion. The grip on her was so tight and so emphatic, that it almost felt re-assuring, and she slowly stopped the convulsions.

The attacker was taller than she and he attempted to say something into her ear, but a last attempt at squirming away necessitated one last squeeze to convince her that she had no hope of getting loose.

The voice was that of an older man and the grip, although quite convincing, momentarily displayed the signs of age, as he had to re-grip her demonstrating some loss of former strength. It was still dark, but for the light emanating from the TV in the den. He said,

"Don't move, don't scream, don't do nothing, understand?"

She nodded as best as possible given the grip he had on her.

She could then hear the sound of duct tape being pulled apart with his free hand and his teeth.

"Damn dentures." He muttered.

After struggling for several seconds, which felt like minutes, he finally got the duct tape undone with his one free hand and began to wrap it around her mouth. He wrapped it around her hair and lips without any hesitation or without asking if it was too tight or too uncomfortable.

After both hands were freed up, he wrapped her arms at the wrist with the tape, behind her back. He took her left hand and examined it. There was no wedding band. He then dragged her to one of the chairs in the living room and sat her down and wrapped up her ankles and proceeded to wrap the tape around her and the chair, like in an old silent movie, where the damsel was tied to railroad tracks awaiting some awful doom. Despite the arcane method of restraining her, it was nonetheless effective. The only visible reaction was in her eyes. He apparently didn't care if she saw him or not, as though he wanted her to see him and realize what this was all about.

She was not a wealthy woman and had no jewelry or other valuables around the house and she began to wonder what he might do if he found nothing of value. He hadn't threatened her with any gun or knife, so she assumed it was a robbery. Something else made her wonder. The only reports of robberies in the past ten years had involved kids. This was certainly no kid.

"Why in the world would an older man be doing this kind of thing?"

There was some light coming through the widow and she saw a shadow, lurking outside. She became more worried, because this guy apparently had an accomplice who was keeping an eye on what was going by on the street. Would they stay longer working as a team? Strangely, she didn't feel threatened for her life, but she certainly wanted this whole thing to end. She kept thinking, if he comes up empty handed, would he torture her? Somehow, she was not worried about any physical harm but for the previous thought. She had a sense that this was a professional job, and not that of some drug crazed kid who was capable of anything.

He was rummaging through things in every room. He was looking for something, but she had nothing of real value. She finally heard the sound of breaking glass in the den, probably in the curio cabinet. She heard him grumble and walk down the hall towards her. She tensed up to waiting for what she felt would be the final encounter, one way or the other.

Then, as he rounded the hall and entered the living room, she finally caught a clear, head on glimpse of her attacker. The pupils in her eyes, already wide from the attack, opened even more so. She knew this guy. She had never seen this guy before, but she knew him. She was now convinced of that. All of the sudden, everything that had raced in her mind up to this point was erased in one fail swoop. He was medium tall, with a huge frame, receding gray hair, broad shoulders, a chiseled jaw and face and the look of an angry man in his eyes. No glasses.

No, she had never seen this man before in person, but he had been described to her and that description has been indelibly etched into her consciousness for the past forty or so years. It was a memory that could never be erased from the mug shot shown her by Detective Ernie Dugan, some thirty years ago.

Just then, another man came storming into the living room. The first guy tripped the second guy and for a moment, she saw both of them together and had a flash of déjà vu. The second man was a much younger man, and he too, looked familiar, but not directly. She had seen him before and she now realized that the second guy had shown her a picture of the first guy some thirty odd years ago, after the explosion, but it couldn't be the same guy. The second guy was too young and the first guy was much younger in the picture.

Oh, it was all coming back to her, like a thirty year-old instant replay, a rerun of a bad dream.

The first guy ran out before the second guy was able to recover. He made a brief attempt to pursue him, but gave up when he saw the engraved locket necklace on the floor leading to the door. Strangely, he placed it in his pocket without saying a word. He then came back to the living room, turned on a light and began to pull the duct tape off. She was wrong... he was not an accomplice. As he completed the unwrapping, she started shaking like a leaf crying. He kneeled down, held her hand and pulled out his wallet and flashed a badge with an official looking photo ID card:

Thomas R. Dugan
Springfield Police Department
Detective

Chapter 19

The Bolero Unravels

When Edison arrived at his mother's house, Detective Carlos Manera was in charge, along with two uniformed policemen. Tom, after calling for a team to come to the house for the investigation, left. He told Dorothy that he was off duty and was just driving by when he suspected something going on and that another on-duty detective would come from the station to take over the investigation.

Edison rushed into the living room and immediately hugged his mother, asking,

"Are you OK?"

"Yes, I'm still a little nervous, but I'm not hurt."

Edison looked her over and was initially satisfied that she was OK and not harmed in any way.

"My god, what happened"

Detective Manera chimed in,

"Well, apparently at about 9:37 PM this evening, Mrs. Barr was assaulted in the kitchen by a yet unknown assailant. Apparently the motive was robbery."

Edison took a quick glance around and since everything at least in the living room looked in-tact, he asked,

"What in the world did he take? The Picasso is on loan to the Smithsonian, isn't it?" He quipped sarcastically.

"Fortunately, while the intruder was rummaging back in the den, an off-duty detective was passing by and noticed something going on." Detective Manera relayed. "The intruder didn't get much time to ransack the house."

The detective motioned to Edison to come with him back to the den. Upon entering the den, Edison saw that the curio cabinet was broken and some of the trinkets were strewn all over the floor. Edison subconsciously knew that something didn't add up, but due to the confusion of the situation, it didn't quite sink in. Instinctively, he walked into the bedroom, and saw that everything was intact and the spare bedroom was also untouched.

Detective Manera told Dorothy and Edison that in the morning, someone from downtown would come out to the house with some mug shots for her to look at, based upon the description she gave him a bit earlier. He continued,

"Let me double check with you on the details, he was Caucasian, about six foot, over 200 pounds, maybe 65 or older, receding gray hair with large hands, although he was wearing gloves. Is there anything you can add?" He asked looking at Dorothy.

"No, officer, I think that covers it." "Remember it was dark and it seemed to happen so fast."

"I certainly understand, Mrs. Barr, but if you should remember anything, please let me know. I'll stop by later tomorrow, after you look at the mug shots." He handed her his business card and asked Edison, "Do you have any knowledge about anyone meeting this description that might have targeted your mother.?"

Edison, not knowing much at all, responded,

"No, I know of no one."

He took Edison aside and asked again,

"This doesn't look like a random burglary. I don't want to further alarm your mother tonight, but can you think of anyone who would want to steal anything your mother has? It is very unusual for a 65 year old to be involved with a house invasion."

Edison hesitated a split second and said,

"No, my mother doesn't keep anything of value in the house, I can't imagine why anyone would think she does."

Detective Manera took notice of the split second of Edison's indecision and made a mental note, jotting a quick note to himself. Edison noted that the detective picked up on his nonverbal response and decided not to pursue it. It was an unstated chess match and both instinctively knew it was something to deal with later.

The police had completed their limited investigation, checking both the inside and outside of the house. The police team left, showing Edison the rear door, which had been pried open with some sort of crow bar and admonished him to repair the lock and install a dead bolt first thing tomorrow. Edison readily agreed and they left.

All of the sudden, a quiet befell the house and Edison once again asked, "How are you feeling, now?"

"I think I'll be OK, but would you just stay with me for awhile, until I settle down a bit?" She asked.

"Don't worry, I'll stay as long as you like. Do you want to come over and stay with me tonight?"

"No, I'm sure nothing else is going to happen tonight. I just need to settle down."

Edison proceeded to the kitchen and made a cup of tea for the both of them. He then asked, without provoking her,

"Do you have any idea why... all this?" motioning around the room.

"I'm still shaking. Can't even think about that, now."

Edison didn't want to press her, although he had suspicions.

"Listen, just drink this and relax." Trying to inject some humor to relieve the tension, he quipped, "Did he as least get that ugly painting back in the spare bedroom?"

"No." she said emphatically, "I like that picture. I don't understand why you don't like it."

They had always disagreed on that painting. It depicted a depression era bar scene from the viewpoint of the piano player showing the somewhat seedy bar in the background and an upright piano with a pair of hands on the keyboard in the foreground.

Edison noticed what was missing from the curio cabinet. Now, Dorothy realized that Edison knew what was missing. Dorothy certainly knew what was missing. The attempt at humor was really Edison's way of letting her know, without making a big deal of it, at least for the time being.

One was an engraved gold locket necklace, which Dorothy always claimed was a wedding gift from Edison's father and the other, a faded color snapshot of a rocky shoreline with a bluish ocean scene. There were no identifying landmarks. Each time Edison had asked her where the picture was from, she always said she didn't know and that it was the very first color snapshot she had ever seen and the view of the ocean just soothed her.

When Edison had checked out the back of the picture, he found an equilateral triangle with the letters RSS under the base of the triangle. Edison always thought it was a mark of some sort with the initials of the person who took the picture. He always thought it was a strange memento, but lots of other people had weirder things, for sure. But now... "there's something more to this picture than meets the eye. Why else would someone commit armed burglary just to get this old faded picture of a rocky ocean scene?" Edison thought. What Edison didn't tell his mother, was that he found the photograph laying on the walkway in front of the house when he was coming in earlier and put it in his pocket.

[MEANWHILE]

The operator was rapidly typing away at the keyboard. A sudden click of the mouse, another click, and then a short pause and the index finger of his right hand imitating a gun, hit the ENTER key. On the screen, data from the house invasion and robbery report came up on the screen, with the heading... Barr, Dorothy.

He then opened the engraved locket necklace he picked up at Dorothy Barr's home. Inside read the following cryptic engraved lettering...

REE OS
OS SS

Love, Artie

CHAPTER 20

Been Mistreated?

Edison got to the store early. It was the big day, the "Road to Fame" auditions concert was scheduled to start at noon and all of the last minute preparations had to be made. Edison just got off the phone with the locksmith, who promised to go out to his mother's house that morning to repair the lock and install a new dead bolt. As he began to get up from his desk the phone rang.

"Good morning, Big Notes, Edison speaking"

"Hey Edison, EC here." Came the voice over the phone.

"Hey back at ya."

"I know it's a week early, but I'm doing a shoot at Tanglewood and we'll be coming through after lunch and thought if you had that new box ready for me to test, it might save some time when I come back."

"Well, I've got all of the electronics done, but I haven't quite got it hardwired yet."

"Can I at least check it out?" "I've got a couple of hours to kill before I can catch a plane out of Bradley."

"Sure, if you don't mind it being temporarily wired together with alligator clips and electrical tape."

"I wouldn't have it any other way." "You know me, I'm not one to stand on formality."

"Well, since you sound so awfully damn accommodating today . . . do ya feel like havin some fun?" Edison asked with a bit of daring attitude.

"You know I do, as long as I've got the time." What's cookin?

"Well, were running our annual open mike audition later." Do ya feel like doin a run through... with an audience? At least you can give the new box a test drive."

"Sure, no problem, I owe you so much, I can't begin to repay you..." he said before being cut off by Edison.

"No, no, that's not what I mean. What would be fun... is if you could come incognito, you know, and..."

"Ah, I get it. Sure, we've got some props here, we can work something out."

"Cool. But let me warn you."

"Yeah?"

"You get no special preferences. You'll be just like any of the others." He said about as sarcastically as he could be.

"I'll take my chances." He chuckled.

"Great, if you hit here about 2, I'll put you on last, then you can just cut out quickly without anyone knowing what hit 'em."

"Works for me, see you at 2."

"Later." Edison said, hanging up the phone with a wry smile.

"Hey boss, do you know where that orange three prong extension cord is from last week?"

"I think it's in the side closet with all the pedals."

Edison felt that he had to at least call Will. Edison would occasionally call Will when 'an event' was about to take place and Will understood that it was always to be low key. Edison knew Will would not want to miss this.

Kate arrived at the store, with a flute case in hand. She had absolutely no intention of actually playing it, but she wanted to get a rise out of Edison, to see his reaction to the possibility. There was a nice size crowd gathering in front of the make shift stage as the noon hour approached and there were plenty of people down the street, viewing exhibits and generally milling around.

All of the performers were working off nervous energy by pacing around and engaging in meaningless chit chat.

"Do you have room for one more performer?" Kate asked wryly with a wink.

Edison sensed this was a ruse and decided to play along.

"Hmm, let's see." You've missed the deadline, but seeing that you're a friend of the family, hmm, how about if I put you on after the... Elvis impersonator... and before the guy playing the recorder?"

"You've got an Elvis impersonator?" Kate asked incredulously.

"I'll find one if you play that damn flute!"

She opened the case and showed there was no flute inside, just her lunch. "How did you know?"

"It was more like a prayer." Edison divulged. "Excuse me, go have a seat if you want, I've got to get things rolling."

Edison proceeded to the microphone in the middle of the stage. There were two side mikes for groups, a drum set, keyboard and a couple acoustic and electric guitars and a base guitar in the background area along with a couple of amplifiers and speakers. Behind the main amp, was a home brew concoction of wires and electronic components held together by alligator clips and black electrical tape. In the entry area of the store were a couple of Edison's most expensive guitars, a Les Pau l and a classic black and white Fender Stratocaster.

"Hello everyone, welcome. I'm Edison Barr, owner of Big Notes and today is our 8th annual Road to Fame audition concert. We have nine, uh, make that ten performers today, (looking at Kate as if to be rubbing it in a bit) who will be showing us their stuff, and if they're any good... and a bit lucky, let me introduce two honored guests who will be listening to see if there's any contract potential here today. First let me introduce Brian Wolfe, owner of the Lyon's Gate recording studios." APPLAUSE " And next, let me introduce Nancy Stuart, talent co-coordinator for Maddman Records, an independent record label out of New York." APPLAUSE "So without any further ado, here's our first act. He's a folk singer from Northampton, and his name is Hank... Singer? Is that right, you've got to be kidding."

"No, it's really my name, no kidding."

"Well, then here is singer, Hank Singer."

Hank sang an original song and did a nice job. The lyrics were rather catchy and well versed and the melody was engaging if not commercial, typical stuff for the Road to Fame, Edison thought, a good start.

Following Hank, were a string of eight performers. The only group of note was the number five group, who consisted of two guys and two women who, obviously influenced by Fleetwood Mac, had a kind of upbeat variation which was refreshing and if not totally innovative, showed some promise in terms of adapting and playing with confidence, or at least as a good cover band. They had the rapport with the audience that it took to make it. Edison noticed that the two guests had jotted down some notes on them. They also got the loudest audience response on the applause meter and were the leaders for the first prize.

About 1:55, an older looking man in a wrinkled beige raincoat with a Burberry plaid liner, wearing dark sunglasses and a brown wide brimmed hat, who apparently had not shaven for more than a few days came walking up to the store's entrance. He was limping slightly and had his hands in his pocket and a cigarette hanging out of his mouth with the ashes hanging on precariously. He finally flicked off the dangling ashes, before entering the store. Edison took notice of him without paying attention to him, shook his head slightly, restraining a laugh and whispered,

"Hey Pops. You look like a flasher."

"Want me to roll up my pants?" he responded, not to be outdone.

Edison just shook his head, chuckling.

"You may have chosen the wrong profession, eh?

As Pops walked into the door, he began to look closely at the two expensive guitars Edison had placed near the door. Mike, one of Edison's employees had been backing up some of the performers on the guitar and considered himself a decent player. When he saw this scraggy looking guy, he announced in a paternalistic voice, "Excuse me, I'm sorry, but these guitars are for serious guitarists."

"Oh, sorry… didn't know." Pops apologized "Is there anything I can use, I'd like to play a couple tunes."

"Are you looking to buy one?" asked Mike half jokingly, trying to hold his disbelief.

"No." Pops said politely, "Just lookin for something to use on the stage."

"Ah, on stage, like now?"

"Here, this one looks like it'll suit my needs." Pops said as he began to pick up the signature Stratocaster, finally disregarding Mike's previous admonition.

"Excuse me mister, but I already…"

"Mike, let the gentleman use whatever guitar he likes."

"But Mr. Barr, that's your…"

"I know, Mike, it's the most expensive guitar in the shop."

Mike was quite miffed, as Edison would not let him use the very same guitar, and he thought, "…and here he's letting this homeless pervert use it?"

"Mike, why don't you back him up with some blues progressions, if he needs it." Edison said trying to console him.

"Ah, come on Mr. Barr, do I have to?"

"Humor me, Mike."

Edison then took Pops by the arm and walked with him up to the stage area as though the old man with needed assistance walking up to the stage while they exchanged some words. He then explained the jumble of wires behind the amp, and Pops proceeded to plug the Stratocaster into the makeshift preamp box and the wires from the box into the Marshall amp.

Edison then announced to the crowd intentionally not mentioning any names,

"Well, everyone, this is our last performer, he's going to do some blues for us, enjoy."

As Edison made the announcement, a lot of people got up out of their chairs and decided to stand, assuming the last act might not be worth staying, so they could make a quick getaway, considering this guy looked like he was homeless. Brian and Nancy, the two talent searchers began to gather their notes in order to get to Edison the second Pops was finished and beat a hasty retreat after the awards were handed out. Pops looked like it was going to be a really low rent imitation of Leon Redbone.

Pops began to do a final tune on the guitar and the hodgepodge of wires with the amp and began to warm up. Pops' fingers flowed over the frets like silk. The effortless movement over the frets and the restrained confidence of his touch was totally out of sync with the environment. After no more than five seconds of warming up, Brian and Nancy reopened their notebooks and started giving Pops and Edison the strangest stare. Most of the crowd snapped their necks and almost gawked in disbelief as he continued to warm up.

Many were disoriented at what they were hearing coming out the amp speakers. Pops was now about a minute or so into loosening up his fingers and all the people down the street at the arts exhibits were suddenly returning to the stage area. Something extraordinary was happening, and everyone in the immediate area sensed it.

The whispering in the crowd asking who this guy was suddenly halted to a total silence as everyone waited to hear Pops say something before he started hoping for some clue to his identify. He didn't say a word. He just glanced at Edison and then nodded and began to play.

The intro was definitely the blues, no pretense, just a riff that if anyone else had played it earlier in the concert, it would've been considered extraordinary, but somehow now, just seemed as though Pops was just working his way into something more, much more. His voice was raspy, but strong, surely the result of too many years of inhaling first hand cigarette smoke.

"Have you ever been mistreated.."
"You know just what I'm talkin about..."

As Pops moved into the next riff, he was bending the notes with so much emotion and ease, that it felt like he was pulling your heart right out of your chest without any anesthesia. By this time, the notes were flowing faster than water over Niagara Falls and his fingers were just sliding up and down the frets as if it were greased lightning. Mike, who had grudgingly and half heartedly agreed to back up this guy, could just stand there, jaw dropped, slowly shaking his head in utter disbelief. "This guy can't be for real." was the only thought he could muster. He was totally emasculated as a self-absorbed guitar player who had no prayer of keeping up with Pops, the homeless guy pervert.

Pops moved into the second verse, but by this time, most everyone in the crowd could barely keep their lower lips from scraping on the ground.

As he finished the first song, he segued right into another, this one equally strong and gut wrenching, equally stunning.

By this time, every window in the area was opened with people nearly falling out, every outdoor vendor had left his or her booth, every pedestrian in the area had gathered around. There was not sole beyond the area of the stage, now easily, close to a thousand people strong, crammed in to hear this sad looking man literally tear up every emotional string in the crowd and on the guitar.

The final flourish of nearly unbelievable notes sequenced at the end, winding down like a Saturn rocket taking off, was like the music version of Picasso.

The final chord hung on the crowd for a couple seconds, while he bended all four strings in the chord. Then a mere two people in the crowd of a thousand actually began to applaud. Most everyone around those two just turned and stared so that the two folded their applause in about two seconds. Applauding this performance would have been like applauding in church or synagogue. When the music from above speaks, you don't applaud. You're humbled, in awe, in silence.

In the few seconds following the last chord, Pops, nearly unnoticed, walked off stage, and told Edison,

"Great sound, Eddy boy, just what I've been looking for. If you could just attenuate the dissonance about 2 to 3 db more, it should be right on the mark."

"You sure?" Edison inquired.

"Oh yeah, you did it again. I don't know how I can repay you, but wire it up and make up the bill, I'll be around in 10 days to collect the box."

"You got it, and thanks for…"

"Thanks nothing, Eddy boy, if you ever need a real favor…"

"You better duck out of here, before they realize what hit them."

Pops shook hands with Edison, slapped him on the upper arm and disappeared around the corner, got in his car with his two associates and left unnoticed by the crowd. Brian and Nancy were almost drooling and caught Edison and asked where Pops had gone, they wanted to talk with him. Sure. Edison informed them that Pops already had a contract and was just there as a favor.

"He wasn't really part of the show, why don't you give me your best performer before Pops." They insisted in confirming who Pops really was, but Edison held his ground. He was after all, dedicated to protecting his clients' privacy.

CHAPTER 21

The Car Napping

Edison wanted a nice quiet meal after the day's activities. Cleaning up and being bombarded with questions about Pops left him drained. He and Mel decided to go their favorite place, the Joy of the Wok for some spicy sesame shrimp and hot garlic chicken. The baby was very active, moving and constantly kicking. Whenever Mel would eat something spicy, the baby seemed to settle down. Mel was convinced she would have to eat spicy Chinese and Mexican food for the duration of her pregnancy. Edison also wanted to fill her in on the details of the break-in at his mother's house. As they were leaving the parking lot at their condo, Edison noticed an older blue Cadillac parked on the street with its dimmer lights on, and nobody in the car. Edison was always torn on what to do in these circumstances, let it go and ignore it or try to see if the car's doors are unlocked and turn off the lights and risk some possible legal hassle. He looked at Mel and she knew what was going through his mind.

"Let it go, it's not your problem."

"But it's an older car and the battery might go dead."

"You don't know. It could be a brand new battery."

"OK, OK." Edison relented and they proceeded to drive to the restaurant.

The parking lot wasn't filled up as it sometimes can be at the Joy and Edison was relieved. Peace and quiet tonight, please is all he could think about. They walked in and were greeted by Frank, the owner.

"Oh, I see little one getting much bigger!" he exclaimed, referring to Mel's expanding midsection. "Now you need two meals, good for business."

"Yeah, we thought we'd get him used to your food early, so he'll want to come back later." Edison joked.

"Where you been with friends?" Frank asked, referring to the fact that Edison and Will would normally come in after tennis during the winter months.

"No tennis in the summer, Frank, now we're doing scuba diving." Edison explained.

"Ah, scuba. Stay away from fish tank, please." He quipped, referring to the large fish tank at the front counter.

"If you insist."

"You sit at usual table in back, OK?"

"Thanks, Frank." Mel agreed.

By the time they settled into their seats, Frank had the server bring two bowls of wonton soup to the table. Frank knew they liked to sip the soup as they pondered their selections on the menu. Tonight, they knew what they wanted, but it was still nice to have the unpretentious attention.

Mel felt like some frozen yogurt after leaving the Joy, so Edison decided to stop at the 7-11 a half a block down the road. Mel wanted something 'disgusting' for dessert, so he stopped the car, left the motor running and told Mel he'd be back in two minutes.

After Edison walked into the store, an older man with a large frame opened the car door with Melissa inside, immediately plopped down in the driver's seat and put the car in reverse, closed the door before she could barely utter a shriek, which she let out, but not before the car was already on the road. The man grabbed her by the scruff of the neck with a force of unquestionable authority and stated,

"Stop the noise and be quiet, if you don't want to get hurt."

Melissa knew he meant business and complied, but couldn't stop herself.

"Can't you see I'm pregnant?"

"Can't you see I mean business?" He quickly responded.

He drove around the corner and stopped the car, put it in Park and grabbed her by the left hand, looking for a wedding band. He was visibly disturbed when he realized that there was none. He looked at her belly and demanded,

"Where's your wedding ring?"

Melissa, still startled, frightened and shaking like a cheap vibrator, mumbled,

"I don't have one." Why do want a wedding ring, I don't have one." she cried in near hysteria.

"Christ, what's this world coming to." He commented in a disapproving voice. "Where's the gold?" he asked in a forceful voice.

"Gold, what gold?" "Jesus, what's the matter with you?" "Let me go... get the fuck out of here."

He looked at her for about five seconds and realized that she indeed knew nothing about any gold. He released her hand and wrist and jumped out of the car and disappeared around the corner into the night as quickly as he jumped into the car, knowing that the news of the encounter would be received by Edison, the one person he wanted to get the message. He didn't care about any police report, same as with the encounter with Dorothy Barr.

This whole incident took no longer than ninety seconds and as Edison was coming out of the 7-11, he got torqued off because the car wasn't there and immediately thought Melissa had taken it to the Dunkin' Donuts store two doors down for some coffee. Not only was he upset at her for disserting him at the 7-11, but they agreed she would avoid the caffeine during the last few weeks of her pregnancy, hoping at least she'd go with decaf. As he began to head toward the donut shop, Melissa pulled into the parking lot, applied the brakes in a sudden stop and nearly collapsed over the steering wheel.

Edison opened the passenger door and was about to give her a piece of his mind, when he realized something was wrong. He got out, ran around to the driver's door, took her out and gave her a big hug and couldn't help but notice she was a wreck.

"My god, what's wrong?" He asked intensely.

Melissa couldn't answer as yet. All she could do was cry and shake, as Edison tried to comfort her. It took nearly five minutes for her to calm down to the point where she could talk.

"This man, this ugly old big man with a jaw that looked like it was made of granite jumped in the car and drove around the corner. He wanted my wedding ring and kept asking me about gold, goddamn gold!"

"Are your alright, did he hurt you?"

"No, I'm OK, he just kept demanding I tell him about the gold… the fuckin' gold.?

"Listen, should I take you to the hospital?"

"No, I'll be OK, he just grabbed my wrist, that's all."

Edison took a look at her wrist. It was a bit red, but nothing else out of the norm.

"He didn't want anything else?"

"No, just wedding rings and gold? What in the fuck is this world coming to?"

Edison instantly knew it was the same guy who had broken into his mother's house. He got the message, but he still wasn't sure what the message meant, but slowly the pieces were starting to come into focus. The description was too close and the event was equally bizarre. "How did he know where we were?" he thought to himself, then it dawned on him it was the blue Cadillac.

At that moment, his tolerance for his mother's silence had just snapped to the point where nothing, absolutely nothing was going to stop him from finding out what in the hell was going on. Other than making sure Melissa and the baby were OK, he was now obsessed with running over to his mother's house had have it out with her. Mel was a doctor, so he believed her when she told him she was OK physically.

CHAPTER 22

The China Syndrome

When Edison arrived at his mother's house, she initially thought he came over to make sure the door had been fixed properly and she was going to thank him for taking care of it. As he came through the door, she knew it was more. He was mad. She could almost see the steam coming out of his eyes.

"Do you know what just happened?" he demanded, fully knowing she had no clue what had just taken place.

"Settle down, can I get you something?"

"No mother, nothing, sit down. Melissa was just accosted in front of the 7-11 while I was getting some ice cream."

"Oh my goodness, is she OK? The baby?"

"Yes, thank God, she's OK." He stared.

"Kids, what are these kids up to today?"

"It wasn't a kid, mother." "You know who it was!" he emphasized.

At that instant, she realized what this was all about. The look on her face said it all. It was the same man who accosted her. It was the same man who had broken into her house, looking for her wedding band and mementos. The same man who blew up her house. The same man whose mug shot picture she saw forty years ago from the detective that questioned her. The same man who had blown up her husband some forty years ago! Harry, (Hacksaw) Elam.

For the first time in his life, Edison felt that his mother would tell him everything he had wanted to hear ever since he was a child.

She held her face in her hands and began to sob. Although it pained her to begin talking, he realized it would be cathartic. She couldn't avoid this any longer. Now, not only was she in jeopardy, now her grandchild was too. This couldn't go on any longer. As she collected herself, Edison went to the kitchen to get her some tea. They were about to have a long talk, a very long talk. Strangely, Edison was just as nervous as she was. He was actually shaking too, afraid to finally face the truth. It had been so long in coming.

"That man is from my past. His name is Harry Elam. They call him 'Hacksaw'. He allegedly sawed off a man's pinky in order to get a ring that he claimed was his. She began hesitantly. He and your father were involved in something, well, not quite proper, back in the mid-thirties, during the depression."

"I knew it, he's a criminal." Edison thought, reaffirming his worst fears all these years.

"Your father was no criminal mind you... he graduated from medical school and wanted desperately to become a surgeon. He had the hands of a virtuoso, but they knew he was too good, better than all of them put together, so they wouldn't let him work, or practice, because they were afraid of him, threatened by him."

"Why?" Edison asked.

"That's not important now, they just wouldn't." "Anyway", she continued, "he had no other choice but to use his hands to make a living. He had such wonderful hands, with long slender fingers. He could play the piano like no one I've ever heard, then or now." She remembered fondly.

Edison, now realizing his passion for music came from his father, "Was he a musician, then?"

"Yes, whenever he could get the work. Remember, it was the depression" "He played with some of the best bands back then, back in Pittsburgh, down there on Liberty Avenue and Wylie Avenue. When I first saw him play there, I didn't care what people said, I just wanted to be with him."

"What was so wrong about that people would've cared?"

"Well," she stammered slightly, "well, he was a... he was a lot older than me. Back then, young girls just do that kind of thing, hanging around smoky bars and saloons."

"You keep using, 'was', is he really dead?" Edison asked hesitantly.

"I might not have told you about him much, but I would never lie to you, yes, as I've told you all along, he is dead."

"What happened?"

"Well, that's where this man comes into it."

"You mean the big guy?"

"Yes, the big guy." "Harry, Harry Hacksaw Elam. He and your father got involved in some nasty business back then. Your father had good hands, he could've been a great surgeon. You know, he could tell whether or not you were lying, just by feeling your forehead or your palm, he had such sensitive hands. That's how he knew how much I loved him, when he touched me." She caressed her arms by herself. "Anyway, sometimes, when they asked your father for help, he always obliged, he just couldn't say no to anyone needing help."

"Help? Help doing what?"

Dorothy sighed, "Breaking into safes, cracking safes, like a common criminal... he was anything but common, though. They would only call him for the really big jobs. He could feel the movement of the tumblers for the combination of a safe faster that it took most people to open them with the combination."

"Does this have to anything with some kind of gold?"

"Well, back on St. Patrick's day, back in the 30's they called for your father. They wanted to open a safe on a train in Springfield coming from New York and Philadelphia and we were in Pittsburgh. To make a long story short, your father was part of a gang that drove up to Springfield and held up that train and he opened the safe for them. Inside was a crate of newly minted gold $20 double eagle coins. I think they were minted either in 1932 or 1933, I can't remember exactly, but it was right after the depression got really bad. The government was recalling all of the gold. They wouldn't admit that a shipment of gold coins was stolen. It could've started a panic worse than already existed at the time so they never prosecuted anyone and the coins were never recovered. All I know is that your father never got anything from that, nothing, I swear.

"So, who's this Hacksaw guy, anyway?"

"Well, he drove the getaway car. He was just a young kid, even younger than me back then and didn't know any better. They traced the car back to him and they sent him to jail for holding up the train. He wasn't the sharpest tool in the shed, if you know what I mean. He was the only one from the gang that ever went to prison for the robbery... I think he was in jail for ten or fifteen years. While he was in prison, he cut off the pinky of another convict and had to stay in prison for another fifteen years. When he got out, he wanted his part of the loot from the robbery. I don't know much else, but somehow, someone duped the other two guys out of the gold coins and made off back to Pittsburgh, where most of them were from, along with your father. When Harry got out of prison he started looking for everyone to get his due. The other two guys in the gang ended up dead. I think Harry must have done it. He then started to accuse your father of stealing the coins, but we never had them. He didn't care."

She started crying big time. Edison tried to console her, but her weeping was unstoppable. Edison didn't press her. He was having a cacophony of emotions himself and needed the time to digest and process everything. He sat there, holding her hand, hugging her and physically consoling her.

After a few minutes, Dorothy tried to continue,

"He... He..."

"He what Ma, did he kill him too?"

"I was out getting some groceries for dinner with you, you were just an infant.. we were walking down the street, you were in a stroller. You were only, maybe three months old. That bastard threw several sticks of dynamite into our house, while your father was still inside, playing the piano." She finally got it out, weeping as she spoke.

"I'm sorry. I just couldn't tell you, I was so ashamed." She admitted.

"Didn't they ever get him?

"No, they could never prove anything. Back then they didn't have the, you know, the labs to find anything. Now, they have DNA and all that stuff, but then, oh my god, there wasn't anything left of the house..."

"Or Dad?" Edison completed the sentence.

"We had to gather up whatever was left and bury the bits and pieces."

"Where?"

"Back in Pittsburgh, he always said he wanted to be buried there, he wanted to go home."

"What was his name?"

"Edward, Edward Arthur Clark."

"His name wasn't Barr?" "How'd that happen?"

"I had to change my name. You just couldn't know what it was like back then. I had to, I just had to change our name and move away, far away to here, in Springfield."

"Why Barr?" Oh, that's right, your maiden name was Barrett, right? Or did you re-marry?

"I could never have done that to your father." "I'll tell you about that another time, it's not that important." She insisted.

Edison was not about to corner her at this time. The first name Edison was obvious, his middle name was his father's name, so he figured the rest was just as explainable. He was so thankful for finally getting to the truth, that he was giddy with relief. All of the wild thoughts throughout his life were instantly dissolved. Edison was always better at knowing the worst truth, than not knowing at all. Edison was in a real quandary. Melissa was at home, naturally stressed out and now his mother in equally tough shape. He felt torn and didn't know what to do. Being in the presence of his mother, well, that seemed to be the path of least resistance. He called Kate, to see if she would go over to their place to be with Melissa. She readily agreed and Edison thanked her profusely. He then called Melissa to check up on her and told her what was going on. Melissa was surprisingly understanding and Edison felt bad that he couldn't be there with her.

Edison then began to connect the dots. All this stuff with Will and the computer must have something to do with this too, although the big old guy certainly didn't seem like he'd know the difference between a computer keyboard from TV. Will said it must be the government doing all the cookies and tags on his accounts. He thought, "Are they still trying to recover these coins, and why do they think I would know anything about them? Maybe they don't know that mother never told me about them... maybe they think father somehow hid them away for me. If they knew he was a doctor, maybe they thought he was the only one smart enough to hide the coins and save them for me, without mother knowing?"

The questions in his mind were now falling from the sky in a downpour. He couldn't process everything rationally. It was just time to console his mother and talk some more tomorrow. He made some hot cocoa for her and she agreed the best thing was to go to bed. He figured that Harry would not be around tonight, but figured he'd sleep over anyway, just in case. In the back of his mind, he hoped he would be foolish enough to try it again. Every so often, Edison's anger would flair up, as it did at Danny's, but this is the first time he thought whether he could actually do bodily harm to another human being, the man who murdered his father, but he had no first hand idea what an imposing threat Harry Hacksaw Elam was like in person.

CHAPTER 23

The Morning After

They slept in a bit longer than normal. Dorothy insisted that she was OK and that Edison go home. She was wiped out and needed twenty-four hours to collect herself and Edison understood. It was about 10:30 and Edison had an urge for a regular cheeseburger and fries from Burger King. He arrived at the drive thru board and just wanted a small portion, so he ordered a kid's happy meal, small cheeseburger, small fries and a small orange drink.

"That'll be $2.19, drive up to the pick-up window." He heard. He got to the pick-up window and was fumbling for the exact change in his pocket.

When he got to the window, the attendant, stated, "that'll be $ 2.19", as he peered into the car. "Hey", he continued unexpectedly, "Where's the kid, I don't see any child under 12 in the car! What are you trying to do, mister, do you need a toy that bad, huh?, the nerve of some people" he chastised as he gave back the change to Edison along with the bag and the drink. Edison wasn't sure whether he felt shocked or embarrassed, so he just pulled out murmuring to himself.

[MEANWHILE]

Hack was just going into the office of George Mackin, Vice President at the New England Federal Bank Trust Department. Hack was wearing a sport coat and slacks, probably the most dressed up he had been in years. He shook Mr. Mackin's hand,

"Good Morning, I'm Harry Barrett. (Dorothy's maiden name) I'm Dorothy Barr's brother. I heard through a lawyer that your bank has some kind of trust. She never knew about it and asked me to check on it. She has trouble getting around these days."

"That's Dorothy Barr. Is that her married name?"

"Yes"

"I don't know how much I can tell you, but let me check our computer records." He began to type in some information, backed up, entered some more data, put his hand on his chin and stared at he screen for about a minute. "I've got a reference number for a Dorothy Barrett, but it's been inactive since the 1960s.

"How much is that reference number?" Hack interrupted.

"Ah, no Mr. Barrett, it's not an amount, it's just a file number referencing a trust that was created in 1962. Unfortunately, it was with our predecessor company, Springfield Bank and Trust." Let me check to see if I can find some paperwork on this. Excuse me for a minute."

Mr. Mackin left the office to check with his assistant.

[MEANWHILE]

*   *   *

The computer screen beeped. He clicked the mouse and the following screen appeared:

REFERENCE: Dorothy Barr, nee Barrett

UGTMA: Edison A. Barr

SOURCE: New England Federal Bank

DEPARTMENT: Trust & Fiduciary

CURRENT BALANCE: $ 1,220,323.52

INITIAL TRUST DEPOSIT: $100,000.00

LAST POSTING: December 31

LAST TRUST ACTIVITY: October 21, 1965

CATEGORY: Annual Fiduciary Fee $ 5,415.95

AVERAGE YR. BALANCE: $ 1,226,726.21

RECORDATION DATE: October 21, 1965

The operator dropped his pencil, paused and simply said, "Damn. Could it be that easy?"

*   *   *

Mr. Mackin returned to the office with a computer print out, identical to the on-screen information received by the operator.

"Mr. Barrett, we do have some information, but I'm afraid I can't tell you anything, without having Ms. Barrett here or unless you have a proper power of attorney signed by her, in order to receive the information."

Hack looked upset and generated one of his classic stares directly into the eyes of Mr. Mackin. Mr. Mackin was stunned by the intensity of the stare and froze for a moment. Hack stood up quickly, grabbed the paper out of Mackin's hand and left with a stare that totally emasculated Mackin.

Hack said simply, but with authority, "Don't move until I've left, or else."

Hack huffed out of the office and out the door of the Trust Department and down the stairs. Mackin, never having dealt with such a threatening exchange, decided that is just wasn't worth calling security. He figured the money and the trust was still secure and thought, "Why should I get bent out of shape over some information."

[MEANWHILE]

The operator hurriedly began to type in a new URL address in his browser on the Wide World Web. He accessed the On Line Hampden County Registry of Deeds and Records. He typed in Dorothy's name, both the married and maiden name, clicked on the trust document box and in a couple seconds, a registered document appeared on the screen...

Indenture of Trust

Dorothy S. Barrett Trust of 1965

In consideration of funds provided to Morris and Libby Barrett, as provided in addendum A attached hereto and incorporated and made a part hereof,

The Grantors, Morris and Libby Barrett:

Inserted trust document showing that $100,000.00 was put in trust for Dorothy Barrett Clark as Co-Trustee in 1965 to become effective upon the death of Arthur Clark, or when deceased, then to Edison A. Clark under the Uniform Gift to Minor's Act., as Beneficiary.

Addendum: Trust Company to maintain Trustee in house.

He was tapping his right index finger on the desk in a quick staccato, staring at the amount in the trust fund. "Hmm, Hmm."

*   *   *

Edison had just closed the web site by clicking on his e-mail program on his store computer, when two hands covered his eyes. He was initially tentative, but slowly took his own hands from his mouse and keyboard and embraced the slender fingers over his eyes.

"Having tuna for lunch, again, eh?"

"One of these days…" she responded.   By the way, hotshot, have you seen your head lately?" "Can you like… like spell R O G A I N E?"

Chapter 24

The Birth of the Blues

Edison and Melissa were lying in bed, watching David Letterman's Top Ten list. Tonight's list was the top ten Broadway Bombs...

10. Opra-homa!
9. Twelve Angry Men... and a Baby
8. Meese!
7. The Diceman Cometh
6. West Side Maury
5. Phantom of the Oprah
4. Katz!
3. Oh Velveeta!

By the time Dave got to number 3, Mel was unable to control her laughter. At the peak of her laugh, she gasped to catch her breath. This gasp however ended with a stone stare. The interrupted completion of the laugh caught Edison's attention, with one eye on the TV and the other on Melissa, he immediately realized that she was not holding her laugh to hear number 2.

At that moment, Edison felt like a bucket of water had just been poured under his right leg. Edison looked at Melissa and she looked at him. At that instant, they both acknowledged to each other with a momentary, yet an all-encompassing connection, that their lives would never be the same.

They had planned, prepared and plotted, but now, they could only muster a momentary frozen stare of disbelief, consisting of one-half terror of the unknown and the other half, relief for the end of the intense anticipation.

Then in an instant, Edison pulled back the comforter and confirmed what he already knew. As Mel wriggled out of bed to put on some clothes, Edison began calling his mother to let her know what was happening. Mel advised him in a very short voice that it might be better to first call the doctor to have him meet them at the hospital.

Not to be outdone, Edison instinctively responded in an equally short voice that it might be better not to get dressed just so she could get undressed again at the hospital. In typical clichéd movie fashion, Edison couldn't locate the doctor's number, even though he had it right there on the night stand under the front right hand corner of the telephone, forgetting that he had also already pre-programmed the number into the speed dial on the telephone, weeks earlier.

Fortunately, there was no traffic. Springfield pretty much expires by midnight. Edison came up to a red light and sat there momentarily debating whether to run the light or wait for it to turn green.

"What are you doing? Run the damn light! If a cop stops us, he can give us a escort to the hospital." Mel screamed.

As a pure sign of middle class, don't upset the system, follow the rules mentality, Edison ran the light and experienced a pang of guilt. He was upset. How could all those years butting up against the establishment, how could all the effort expended in changing the system in both undergrad and grad school have brought him to the point where he would actually feel guilt about running a red light on the way to the hospital for the birth of his first child.

"My god, what has happened to me?" Edison thought. Along with the cacophony of other emotions shooting through his mind, Edison was very disturbed by this apparent capitulation to a rigid adherence to middle class mores.

As they finally drove up to the entrance to the Baystate Medical Center, Edison was surprised at the amount of activity, being so late or actually, so early in the morning. The scene reminded him of the Strip in Las Vegas in the middle of the night. The hospital, in an attempt to service its patients better, a predictable byproduct of the push for implementation of quality management, had valet service and a reception area like the Ritz Carlton in Boston. Curiously, there were dozens of people scurrying about, some hospital personnel, some unknowns, but not one person seemed interested in helping them unload the car and assist in checking in at the entrance. So much for quality management. They both found it incredibly surreal that is was so busy at such a late hour, much like Times Square on a Saturday night at midnight, yet so totally unorganized. They then joked that yes, the chaos is indeed like Times Square at midnight.

The reason for the commotion became painfully clear when they tried to check in at the admissions desk. The line. The line!? You know, the line - at the check-out counter... one clerk, one register, K-Mart, Christmas Eve, everyone in a maddening rush, certainly a poster picture for shopping rage waiting to happen line!

Edison swore he heard on the PA system, "Price check at register 1," the collective moans from the patrons in line and that the lady being waited on was writing a check and was fumbling in her purse, the size of Rhode Island, to find a pen and to boot, was asking how much cash back she could get.

"We've got broken water here!" didn't work. The immediate stereophonic response was, "Wait your turn, please!" Although the wait in line probably didn't exceed five minutes, it seemed like forever, like waiting for your bags to be checked at the airport security when you've just heard your flight as "Final call for boarding!" blares out over the PA system.

When they finally were able to check in, they discovered there were 'no rooms at the inn' tonight. Mel sarcastically opined that if Letterman had even better material by number 6 or 7, she would've been here earlier. The receptionist merely kept mumbling, it's a full moon, it's a full moon, why did I take a shift with a full moon. With some two dozen birthing rooms at the hospital, not one was available.

They led Mel and Ed to a waiting area, sort of a triage for impending first birth parents. One by one, all the other couples were escorted to their birthing rooms. It was as though Henry Ford had left his personal imprint on the mass production of babies, except here there were leftover parts, without a car to accommodate them. As if the ER of birthing wasn't enough, the real treat came when we were told that Mel's OB was not available and that a pinch hitter was coming in for the for bottom of the ninth… score tied and with the bases loaded.

Apparently, due to the full moon, there were SRO conditions that night. Mel began to slip into her sarcastic mantra.

"Great, nine months ago I had sex and now I'm finally getting fucked." Hearing that, Edison knew he'd better engage his diplomacy to find them a room before the contractions really began to take over. A sympathetic RN's response made Edison's eyes light up. Apparently there was the V.I.P. room which is always held for, well, V.I.P.s, but was hardly ever used due to a lack of genuine V.I.P.'s in the local area. Apparently a local benefactor donated the money for the larger than normal room, but insisted it only be used for special occasions. The RN assured Edison they could have it at least for the night, but would have to vacate before the supervisor came back on duty the next morning.

Mel was finally wheeled into the V.I.P. birthing room. Wanting the full experience up to now, of natural childbirth, she quickly piped up,

"I'll have that epidural, now, straight up, with a Demerol chaser."

Kristin, the RN cautioned,

"They only come in shots."

"Bring it on." Mel responded without missing a beat.

Dorothy sheepishly edged her way into the room, very nervous and very out of character, unable to make any eye contact with Edison or Mel. Edison told her not to worry, that everything was going fine, but for some inexplicable reason, she continued to be extremely figgity, even to the point of biting her nails and crossing and uncrossing her arms and pacing, as though SHE was the expecting father.

She kept trying to begin to tell Edison something, sort of like a child trying to explain to a parent as to why there were no more cookies in the jar after being told not to eat anymore before dinner. She kept using different words on several occasions, but each time she cut it short and just shook her head, mumbling to herself.

Suddenly after two and a half hours of stable beeping from the fetal monitor and Mel gloriously mellow on the best legal drugs available for the event, all hell broke loose. The monitors started beeping furiously like Geiger counters, as though the mother lode of a uranium find had just been discovered in the room. The RN began paging for the OB, but no response. She immediately ran out into the hall to find a resident. Mel and Ed were clueless, but now, even the drugs couldn't calm down Mel. No one was providing information as four youngish med-school types came dashing into the room.

"Where is in the hell is the OB?" yelled a frustrated RN.

Edison finally took action during a sigh from the RN asking pointedly,

"Please, what is going on, we need information, she's a doctor."

The RN finally relented,

"The oxygen in the placenta has dropped off the chart and if we don't get this baby delivered within the next couple minutes, we could have brain damage... could be a twisted cord or something... where in the hell is the doctor?!?"

Before she finished the statement, two orderlies began grabbing the monitors and pushing the gurney bed into the hallway and down to the OR. Mask ties, bed sheets and lab coats were all flapping furiously while the gurney was being pushed to the OR like a bed race during a homecoming football game or an old Marx Brother's movie. Edison was instructed that he would have to don surgical garb if he wanted to be present for the birth.

Dorothy, slowly paced down the hall covering her mouth, with a small tear oozing out of her left eye. She paused several times as if though thinking about turning back or taking an exit.

At the last possible moment, the pinch hitting OB finally showed up in the OR and took charge, much to the relief of the resident, who clearly did not want to be in charge of this delivery, under these circumstances. Edison wanted to give the OB a few choice words, but certainly restrained himself. There would be time later. Nonetheless, Edison couldn't stem the flow of all of the horrific images of a mentally damaged baby, child and adult. Anger with the doctor, disbelief that this could happen after all the precautions taken, no alcohol, all the pre-natal supplements taken, all the physical care taken, the ultrasound, the perfect record of doctor appointments. An immediate mental reinforcement that even if something horrible happened, he was up to the long term challenges, no matter what, but now I can't even think of such of thing, it won't happen, you son of a bitch.

Mel was now screaming…"As god is my witness… I'll never have another child as long as I live! I need more drugs! And tie my tubes immediately after this thing is out!"

Edison's jaw slowly and uncontrollably dropped in anticipation, as the head slowly emerged. There was a tuft of dark wavy hair, then a head… push, push, we've got to get this baby out immediately… push… push… eyebrows, eyes, a nose, a mouth, a neck… all there… all dark bluish almost purple… Edison hadn't expected this…he wasn't prepared for this… the movies never showed this part… a rush of nausea. Fortunately, Mel couldn't see what was happening… a torso, arms, the twisted cord, looking like dried blood, bluish, bluish, purple… hands, a penis, legs, feet, all dark blue.

Just as Edison was about to lose it, the OB let out a sigh, which strangely calmed Edison down as stifled staccato cries began to fill the room.

"Dad, do you want to cut the cord?"

Edison, being in near shock responded,

"No way, get this done, is he OK?" The nurse placed a while skull cap on his head, and they immediately began testing for responses. Edison wasn't sure what was going on, and nobody was providing any information, but during the next thirty-seconds, the longest half minute of his life (Einstein was right, time is relative) the baby's head and torso began to change color as though the dark blue was being flushed out towards the extremities of his fingers and toes.

Edison experienced an ESP type connection with his son, for at the same time, his fears and anxiety began to flush simultaneously. A confident "Five by five by five!" was proclaimed by the nurses, followed by a collective sigh. They all took a deep breath and relaxed.

Edison immediately piped up,

"What does that mean... is everything OK???? Please???"

"Dad, you couldn't ask for anything better. We evaluate the baby for three different responses and reflexes and five is the best. He scored five for ..., five for... and five for.... You've got a healthy baby boy!" They placed a tag around his wrist.

The nurse then asked Edison if he wanted to hold the baby. Edison paused for only a moment, but the nurse, sensing a bit of uneasiness assured him it would just fine to hold his son. The OB was finishing up and Mel wasn't even aware of what was going on.

"Make sure you get the placenta to the lab for an immediate evaluation, stat, barked out the OB.

Quickly, Edison carefully held his son, under a white heat lamp. He gazed intently into his eyes, which were surprisingly open and wandering around, like trying to ask... "Where in the world am I... this is not where I've been for the past few months... this is new... cool stuff to look at." Edison carefully brought the baby close to his face and whispered,

"I'm here for you. I'll always be here for you, my son. Look at my face and never forget me, no matter what, I'm your daddy and you're my little boy. I can't believe you finally arrived in my life. Remember though, no matter what, never forget this moment, never forget me, never. I'm your Daddy, don't you ever forget that. I'll be here for you no matter what. I'm not going anywhere. I'll be there for your first day of school, your first bicycle ride, your first baseball game and your first girlfriend, well, maybe I'll leave that for you! I'm your family tree, I'm your Daddy, I'm your Daddy." It was the most precious hug Edison ever experienced.

Weeks ago, Edison had a dream, that minutes after being born, his son began talking to him. This baby wasn't talking, but Edison was overwhelmed with a sense of surprise and almost disbelief, that the nonverbal reactions of his eyes and arms, indicated that he somehow understood Edison, and somehow embraced the emotion of the words Edison spoke. Edison knew that he understood, incredible as it sounded. For a second, Edison dismissed the feeling as his personal projection of his incredible emotion of the moment, but the disbelief dissipated immediately and he was indeed overwhelmed with the certainty that this five minute old baby got it, somehow got it, with his innate intellect, his previous incarnations and yes my DNA is in you, our DNA, you do get it!

Within a minute or so, when the nurses finished with her, Edison gave the baby to Mel to hold and they all wheeled back to the VIP room at one-tenth the pace of going to the OR. It suddenly dawned on Edison, "Where's mother?" Edison without intending it or even being conscious about it, perceived Dorothy was avoiding him, avoiding Mel, avoiding the baby.

After arriving back at the VIP room, Dorothy, who had been spying on the VIP room, waiting for them to return, looking for some type of non-verbal indication from Edison and Mel and they came down the hall and into the room from the OR.

Dorothy edged into the doorway of the VIP room, being very nervous, tries to peek around the corner, then pulling back into the hallway, like a nervous and figgity pre-teen girl not wanting to see or be seen by the boys at their first dance. Somehow, she just couldn't seem to bring herself to face anyone in the room, including her first grandchild. Strange.

Dorothy finally took a deep breath as though she were preparing herself to jump into a cold swimming pool. She moved toward the baby and refused to make eye contact with Edison or Mel. She kept her eyes closed.

Edison caught a glimpse of Dorothy and encouraged her in no uncertain terms,
"Get in here and meet your grandson. Don't worry, everything is fine. He has ten fingers, ten toes and all the other parts are fine too."

"Oh my God, that's not what worries me." Dorothy murmured. She opened her eyes, while biting her lip. As she slowly opened her eyes, she squinted, pulling her lips back as though she was afraid of what she was about to see and was avoiding the inevitable as long as possible, and then, seeing the baby, she quickly let out a sigh of relief that could be heard half way down the hall, "Oh my!... He's not....he's beautiful." after glancing at Will, who had arrived just minutes ago.

CHAPTER 25

Tie a Yellow Ribbon

Later that morning, Kate came by with a gift for the baby. It was a video called Baby Songs. Kate said,
"My cousin just loved this. He watched it over and over for about a year. Trust me, you'll even get hooked."

Mel and Edison were still undecided on his name and had narrowed it down to Michael or Evan, but now Mel was annoyed because Edison was advancing a new name out of nowhere, Arthur, his middle name. At first she thought he was joking around, but soon came to realize that he was serious. They had spent time throwing around even comic names that go with Barr. Kate reminded them that since it was a boy, Candi Barr was out and that either Michael, Evan or Arthur would make for a distinguished name, much better that Mars or Hershey, too. Then again, there was always Granola or Crow.

Right then, Dorothy chimed in and broke the gist of the conversation,
"Let's get down to it and stop this foolishness. The birth certificate needs to be filled out and you've got to choose a R E A L name. Mel insisted on Michael and Evan and they then agreed he would be Evan Michael Barr, officially.

Kate, Will, Edison and Dorothy decided to grab some food down in the cafeteria, since Evan was sleeping and had already left his first 'night deposit' consisting of a sticky tar type residue. The nurse joked that this would be the first of many, many diaper changes they could expect after leaving the hospital. They headed for the elevator.

The relief from the stress of the birth became short lived when Dorothy let out a muffled shriek pointing down the hall, when the elevator door opened on the third floor to pick up a couple people. Down the hall and fortunately unable to see them was Harry Elam, leaning against the wall next to a patient room, staring intently at his watch. In reaction to his mother, Edison also realized the genesis of the reaction just as the door was closing, while Kate and Will were in the dark. They looked at each other as all the joy of the previous few hours was immediately dashed. As they sat down to sandwiches and salads, they knew they had to do something. They couldn't chance being seen by Hacksaw in the hospital and jeopardizing little Evan Michael on his first day of life. They decided that take out... back at the room would be best and carefully got a tray and headed back to Mel's room. What in the world was he doing in the hospital, now, of all times was the unspoken question on all of their lips.

*   *   *

Harry was impatiently waiting outside the room of his son, Roger while he was undergoing tests of a personal nature. Harry was not the type to hang around the room and be involved with those types of things going on, even though he visited his son every day, rain or shine, neither dark of night or sleet, etc.

Roger was diagnosed eighteen years ago with Multiple Sclerosis at the age of 32. Roger's wife had left him long ago and Harry was his only living relative. Roger's condition had slowly but methodically deteriorated to the point where he needed on-going surgery and they didn't have any usable health care insurance.

For an old guy, Hacksaw still has a strong constitution and excellent distance vision. That perq just isn't generally available to members of Harry's profession. Harry was in desperate need of money to provide the necessary funds to go through the procedures to alleviate his only son's pain and to make him as comfortable as possible. Harry doesn't like to be under pressure and tends to overreact when things are out of his control.

Edison didn't know that Harry was a walking time bomb who could explode at any time to protect his own son, especially when he believed he got screwed and had money coming to him for his nearly thirty years in prison with nothing to show for it. Edison didn't realize Harry's motivation for his recent exploits and for what could come.

Edison and Dorothy agreed they would not tell Mel about seeing Hacksaw just one floor down and they decided to take the elevator at the far end of the wing in order to avoid any possibility of running into Hacksaw. Will and Kate were curious about the old guy, but realized it would be better to wait awhile after they left the hospital to talk with Edison.

Like most conspiracies, they are only as strong as their weakest link and by the chalky look on Dorothy's face when they returned to Mel's room might have been enough to tip off Mel, but when she said she couldn't even think of eating after seeing that face... well, Mel put the pieces together. Her eyes were like lasers focused on Edison. She was not about to be subjected to that monstrous cretin again and now, it also included a newly acquired maternal protective laser blast.

Edison had the inevitable epiphany about this whole situation and looked at Kate and asked

"Would you let me into the lab this afternoon?"

Kate was caught completely off-guard.

"Why in the world would Edison want to go to the lab... especially today?" She pondered. She let out a hesitant, "Sure... why not?" Hoping to get the inside scoop as to what was going on.

The nurse came in and informed Mel that she was taking the baby for some tests and would be back in fifteen minutes and that she was welcome to see what was going on in the maternity area, as there were a lot of other babies being processed and if she wanted to see all the other babies, to check on Evan's new little friends.

Mel decided she wanted to rest in bed for awhile and quickly dozed off, having been up all night.

About a half hour later, Mel awoke and immediately rang the room bell summoning the nurse. "I want my baby back now."

"He's being cleaned and being tested. Don't worry, he'll be back shortly."

I want my baby, now... she reiterated, I'm not waiting another minute."

When the nurse didn't immediately react, Mel began to struggle out of bed.

"OK, OK, I'll go see if I can speed things up. I'll be back in two minutes."

After two minutes and one second... Mel rang the bell again... then again.

The nurse returned and stammered,

"We're having a slight problem. Evan's not in his bin. I'm positive he's with Linda, the pediatric nurse, who had him a few minutes ago, but we can't find her. Please don't worry. Nothing can happen with our ID system."

Edison left with her and they disappeared around the nurse's station. As they opened the door to the employee lounge, they found Linda nibbling on a tuna wrap and sipping on a Diet Coke.

"Where did you leave Evan?" they asked in unison.

"I just left Evan in his bin, not five minutes ago. Isn't he the cutest little thing?" I can't remember having so many babies all at once in here, isn't it great?" Linda offered, while a piece of shredded lettuce clung to her mouth, as she brushed a napkin to remove it. Little Evan Michael was not in his bin.

CHAPTER 26

Everyone's Worst Nightmare

Upon closer inspection, there was something in Evan's bin... "YOU KNOW WHAT I WANT. I KNOW WHAT YOU WANT" read the hastily scribbled note in a broken, uneven handwriting on a hospital notepad lying in the bin where a six hour old baby should have been.

The first call went to the on duty nurse supervisor, who in turn called the head floor nurse, who in turn called the head of security who in turn called the chief administrator, who in turn called the Springfield Police department, who in turn called the Massachusetts State Police. The troops were mobilized, while everyone tried to put on an air of matter-of-factness they preferred to call professionalism or otherwise referred to as "there's got to be an rational explanation for this...", "nothing like this could happen here" - masking their unspoken terror. Every available security guard was called and posted at every entrance and the internal communications system was erupting with orders, questions and commands.

The high tech security system sprung into action. It would envelope any would-be sophisticated professional kidnapper, or emotional baby thief, but ineffective against a sublimely low tech Harry Hacksaw Elam. A Hacksaw goes right under the radar... and out the automatic service door, used for the convenience of the delivery trucks, where small packages on dollies and rough looking delivery guys go in and out without so much as a trace... but for the video surveillance camera.

CHAPTER 27

Out for Delivery

The Springfield police and the Mass State Police along with hospital administrators, nurses and hospital security supervisors were running around like keystone cops not sure of protocol or if there even was an actual abduction. Nothing had ever happened like this as far back as anyone could remember and sadly, there were never any exercises to prepare for such an event.

Detectives, agents and a crew of techies were ordered to cast a net around the area using all monitoring devices, computers, electronic ID tags and check points. Kate even called and asked her detective brother, Tom to help out, and was surprised how readily he agreed to get involved. In the past, he had steadfastly refused to mix his professional life with the requests of his family and friends.

When detectives tagged and bagged the handwritten note, they approached Melissa and Edison to inquire who might have had a motive to kidnap their newborn. Melissa was borderline hysterical at this point recounting the episode with Hacksaw, while a young black resident tried to convince Melissa to take a sedative, which she adamantly refused... "I don't need any fucking meds... I need my son... what kind of Mickey Mouse operation are you idiots running here? Let me out of here. Edison, be a man and find my son. Kate, get my clothes, I'm going out to look for my son!"

"Melissa, you're not dressed, I'll go gather up your clothes."

"I don't give a shit about any clothes, let's get out of here!"

"You haven't been cleared for release yet." intoned the resident.

"Try to stop me... what are you, a first year resident? I'll bet you got into med school on affirmative action. Out of my way before I insert that stethoscope of yours in a part of your anatomy you haven't even learned about yet!"

"Mel, calm down and let the police do their jobs. Just what do you plan on doing that the police aren't doing right now?" offered Edison.

"Don't tell me to calm down... this is all your fault!" I'm going to find that bastard and cut his testicles off... someone get me a dissecting tool." retorted Melissa. "I'm going to see my lawyer cousin to make sure you aren't allowed anywhere near Evan when I find him, what a fucking nightmare."

Just as she was leaving the room, Tom of all people came walking down the hall with little Evan Michael all wrapped up in a white cotton blanket, with his little white cotton knit cap.

"I was outside checking on delivery trucks on a hunch and we found him in a FedEx delivery truck parked outside the service delivery gate. The driver was returning to his vehicle after dropping off some packages and we found the baby bundled up on the passenger seat, with this note attached... 'I'll be back. Next time for good.' I'll be taking this note for evidence and testing, but I presume this is the work of Harry Elam, but we're holding the driver for awhile to see if there is any chance he was involved, but I doubt it. I'll let you know when I find something concrete."

Melissa pulled Evan to her clutch and started sobbing and fondling him all over to make sure nothing was wrong. "Come here baby... I'll take care of you." She then placed Evan on the hospital bed, proceeded to unwrap the baby and give him a thorough physical examination, making sure all the parts were in perfect order. "Thank God you are OK... just not quite as pink as I would expect, but OK. Edison Barr, I don't want you anywhere near us until you find that monster... I'll be staying at my cousins and don't even think about coming over. I'll have her bring my stuff over from the apartment. She then rushed out of the room and Edison started to follow, but Tom grabbed his arm...

"Maybe you should let her calm down a bit before you see her." All Edison could think was...

"What a nightmare is right, indeed, as though his first conversation with his son was already becoming eerily prophetic."

CHAPTER 28

No Options, No Holds Barred

Edison knew, after being subjected to Melissa's outburst, that there was only one option, and he called Kate and Will to meet him at the store. He was absolutely crushed at the prospect at not being able to even see his son, yet he knew somehow, he, along with his mother was at the intersection of this perverse chain of events seemingly dating back to his father, a man he never knew, let alone remembered.

Edison opened up, "I need your help to pull this off."

Will responded, "I don't think I like this. What exactly do you mean by... pull this off?

Edison continued, "Kate, how much do you personally know about induced ancestral memory replication?"

"No, Ed, you can't be serious?", Will interrupted.

"Kate, please?"

"Ed, just what do you know about that? This is starting to sound weird like our conversation at your birthday party. And what the hell does this have to do with the kidnapping?... and who is the big guy?"

"Kate, before opening Big Notes... I... well dabbled in genetic research while in grad school."

"What Ed is trying to say, is that he almost killed himself in grad school experimenting with hallucinogenic compounds trying to replay embedded memories from his ancestors he thinks is kind of recorded in his DNA somehow.

He had this thesis that life is nothing more than the summation of the continuous emotions experienced by a human being between birth and death and that all of the knowledge, memories and experiences of a human being represented by those emotions is somehow chemically embedded or recorded like a tape recorder somewhere in the DNA chains that are replicated in one's child at conception. The only trick is how to chemically or electrically tap into that region and how to interpret and get that data up to our consciousness or in some other recognizable format."

"Are you fucking serious, Ed?" Kate responded.

"Well, that's not the whole story, but essentially…"

"What in the hell are you doing selling guitars, my god, you're talking Nobel Prize territory here for crying out loud!"

"Maybe, but he almost killed himself using various variations of a basic LSD compound. Needless to say when his Ph.D. dissertation chair found out about it, he thought Ed was using his research as a cover for being a spaced out druggie and threatened to kick him out of the program if Ed didn't withdraw voluntarily."

"Ed???"

"Well, if you really check out the basic composition of LSD, with the right concentration and a usable catalyst, it really tends to open up the subconscious, which is where these memory recordings have to be directly embedded. That's why we all experience deja vu at one time or another."
"Besides… it was kinda hard to employ the double blind scientific method using LSD as a test sample… especially back then."

"And do you think that what we're doing down at the lab with the mice… just what are you thinking about here?" Kate asked pointedly.

"Ed, you can't be serious about this."

"Listen, I've been doing a lot of modeling on the computer in my spare time... I mean these desktop computers today are more powerful than the room size supercomputers I used back in school. I've identified two basic combinations that really should act as the catalyst without the negative repercussions of a standard dose of LSD. I'm convinced if you embed a modified form of LSD presented in conjunction with a complementary antidote in an atomic buckeyball type carrier, a chemical conduit should be created to allow a pathway for the compound to connect the DNA and the subconscious and hopefully reflect that impulse and connect with the DNA sidewall region associated with memory without the hallucinogenic effect. The buckeyball should maintain the integrity of the carrier impulse and bring it to the conscious level with minimal neurologic loss."

"This is not just for my personal curiosity anymore. I need to get some answers about my father. It's the only way I can get my son back. That Hacksaw guy is not about to leave Evan or me alone and without some information I know nothing about, but has got to be somewhere recorded in my DNA. No one else can do this, no one. Not even my mother knows what happened back then. I just need access to some compounds... I saw what I need down at the lab, Kate, Will... can you help me? Listen, I could synthesize this stuff in a matter of hours and if I keep the dosage down below the low end of around 10-15 micrograms, it might just work. Listen, Will, you know how close I was back at school. Let's face it, I don't have any options, here."

"I think the key to this thing is the convergence of quantum physics and genetics. Recent research seems to confirm the existence of the quantum 'twin'. A particle has a mate which has a connection which somehow stays in communication with its twin irrespective of time and space, as we know it. All I need to do is to establish the link between the embedded memory in the DNA chain and the conscious receiver in the brain so that it can be 're-played' through the visual ocular system. The problem with LSD-25 and its derivatives is that the brain's visual system is not in sync with the format of the embedded memory in the DNA, which is why you get the uncontrolled psychotropic experience instead of a true reflection of the embedded memory. Now that's just the first challenge, because if my theory is generally valid, then the embedded memories of the grandparents and their parents and so on and so on are also embedded deeper into the DNA and so you also have to deal with exponential layers of embedded memories, too. Hopefully, though, that will only be an issue of dosage. In this case, all I need to do is to kind of scrape off or get the compound to intereact with the electromagnetic weak force to attach to the first layer of my DNA with my father's memories at the shallowest level and connect that energy back to the visual section of the brain, minimizing loss and distortion. That's where the buckyball fullerine should do the trick. That should keep the integrity of the twin in-tact until it is received in the brain. Well, that's it in the proverbial nutshell. What do you think?"

"You are cognizant that this is like, really FRINGE?" Kate shook her head in near disbelief.

"Naturally."

"But damn, really logical, maybe even syllogistic, bordering on being cool. Count me in." Kate said partly for intellectual curiosity, the other for any additional time spent with Edison.

"I don't think I'm going to be able to talk you out of this?" Will queried in a fence sitting tone of voice.

"I don't have a choice. I would have done it eventually in any case, and you know what I'm talking about, but there is no longer any choice, now. If I don't come up with some answers quick, God knows what that deranged idiot will do to my son."

Kate assumed a posture of resignation, covering her mouth with her hand while she squeezed Edison's left wrist, gazing obliquely at his ring-less finger, biting her lower lip.

"Let's do it." Edison exhorted.

*   *   *

D-lysergic acid diethylamide micrograms, psilocybin, psilocin mescaline. 25 micrograms… 20-80 dosage 50 milligrams is considered standard dosage.

Switzerland in 1938.. circulatory and respiratory stimulant. Structural relationship to a chemical found in the brain

350 paper designs since 1975 milk as a non=specific antidote

CHAPTER 29

Formula One

"If anyone feels this is too far out and wants to back out, I certainly understand and won't think any less of you for not wanting to be involved with this." Edison stated in his best legalese disclaimer voice, after everyone assumed their positions.

No one budged.

"Ed, each of us here has engaged in research albeit ancillary to what you're trying to do here, but we're all dealing with knowledge – how it is acquired - how it is transferred – if and how it might be inherited... so this genetic theory is potentially seminal to what we're doing here. Besides, each of us has probably known someone who's popped some acid at one time or another. If you're going to do it to yourself, it's probably best to have us here to deal with any repercussions and deal with it, head on.

"OK then, I'm going to start with a 10 microgram dosage coupled with a 4 ounce component of milk in 10 minutes, as a non-specific antidote to temper the initial impact." Depending upon the initial reaction, I will increase the dosage in two increments up to a maximum accumulated dosage of 25 micrograms. Keep the recorder going at all times, no matter what. Each of you know your roles?"

Everyone nodded.

"Any questions?"

Will responded, "Yeah, I've got a million of them... Will it make any difference?"

The following are the possible manifestations:

Flash of bright color across the visual field of both
Sheet of light and disappear as a mist
Geometric figures come and go
Sparkles, visual fireworks, busts, hundreds at a time
Lattices, doughnut shaped images, large blobs
Patterns arising from no known primary stimuli
With eyes closed, entopic stimuli normally, may be induced from gentle pressure of the closed eyelid
Sprinkles of colored light when nose rubbed or after coughing
Halos under photopic conditions, around researcher's arm and head, mist around the telephone, difficulty differentiating halos and mists
Stable objects appearing to move, wave or jump, mostly in the peripheral visual fields
With mild digital pressure on the eye, visions of a Mickey Mouse cartoon
Intensified colors lasting a few seconds
Macropsia, perception of object larger than reality, lasting a few seconds
Micropsia, smaller, feet looked like miles away
Negative after images, seeing complementary color of primary stimulus, seeing yellow between blue lines
Trailing phenomena... like a comet trail
Flashbacks, a week or more following last exposure

Higher percentage of
Geometric
Peripheral
Flashes of color
Intensified colors
Trailing
Imagistic
Purification and crystallization

Lasted up to two hours
Distorted vision, as if curved mirror

Edison took a piece of banana with the crystallized compound embedded within it and ingested it.

In about twenty minutes Edison began to experience with his eyes closed with a black face mask covering his eyes, a mist consisting of minute sparkles, not unlike the formation of a solar system from minute specs of mass of cosmic dust.

"So far there are no color distortions or geometric patterns." Hopefully the mist will coalesce into some form of recognizable visual images."

The researchers were relieved to see that Edison was still lucid.

Several minutes later, without any intervening observations, Edison added,

"The mist is starting to assume some rounded shapes and the sparkles have disappeared. Wow, now I'm seeing some shooting things, kind of like the final sequence in 2001 Space Odyssey."

Immediately their faces became rigid, similar to a typical Spielberg shot of the reactors faces instead of the protagonist.

About seven minutes later, Edison began to cry as a swelling tear began to fall from his left eye.

"Edison, talk to us, what's going on."

"Nothing, damn it, nothing." He responded. "It's regressing now and its starting to fade. It's not working. No need for the milk."

Edison took off the eye guard and immediately went for the supplemental dosage.

"Edison, it's too early for that, c'mon now, you know the drill." Kate stated firmly.

"I need to push this thing, I really thought things would coalesce, but it needs just a little bit of a push."

"Yeah, just like a cocaine head." She retorted.

"Please."

"Please nothing. Nothing more until Dave does the tests on you."

"OK." Edison relented.

Dave ran the basic physiologic tests and everything was within normal parameters, and without any apparent immediate neurological impact.

"I'm adding 10 more micrograms." Edison announced as he quickly inhaled the chunk of banana before anyone could object.

He settled down on the bed and made sure the eye coverings were complete.

This time only twelve minutes passed and when an effect took place, Edison was encouraged, knowing the cumulative and regressive characteristics of LSD type compounds.

"Maybe this will push it through." He thought to himself.

"Edison, talk to us, guy, what's going on."

"Eerily similar to the initial mist, but its coalescing faster with slightly brighter colorations, blues…yellows… , but nothing else."

Mike whispered to Dave,

"Blue and Yellow... negative afterimages with complementary colorations."

Dave reacted, "Yeah, more in the zone of the published research."

They remained quiet in order not to disturb Edison in any way.

Ten more minutes passed, no observations from Edison.

"Edison, anything, you've been quiet now for 10 minutes."

Edison reacted as if surprised.

"Ten minutes? Boy, I could have sworn only a minute or two had passed. Nothing."

Two hours total had elapsed since the initial ingestion and if something was going to happen, it would have by now.

"Is it time?" Edison asked in a resigned tone.

"Yeah, sorry."

"I can tell it's fading anyway, interesting attempt, though." Edison stated as though he just completed the first iteration of a multiple sequence regimen, trying to hide his disappointment.

Kate could see this and gave him a significant hug, which lasted about two or three seconds longer than a conciliatory gesture.

Edison then announced,

"I'm going to try the alternative B compound in 24 hours, that should allow enough time to elapse to minimize any cumulative effect."

"Be sure to ingest at least a liter of milk tonight." Dave cautioned.

Kate then announced,

"Let's go, I'm your designated driver.", causing Julie to comment to her with a clear sarcastic tone,

"He's got a baby, now, too."

CHAPTER 30

A Sharper Image

Edison asked Kate to stop at the Big D supermarket on the way home after.

"You should never go shopping on an empty stomach, mister." Quoted Kate flatly without being trite.

"I know, you're right, and when you're right you're right... we'll stop by the DQ for a Blizzard on the way, my treat. I could sure use a Butterfinger Blizzard, and you I might add, looks like you could use one too, but just a small one." Edison announced, as though he was the source of this profound idea. "Besides, there must be at least some milk by-products in the soft serve, no?

"Great idea." Kate reassured him, smiling to herself. "Sounds like a plan."

"One small Butterfinger Blizzard and... do you want one too?

"Actually, I'll just have small cone... half and half."

"OK, one small Blizzard... Butterfinger and one small cone twist. Will there be anything else?"

"No, that'll do it."

"That will be $3.18, please."

"Here's a five."

She punched the cash tendered into the computerized cash register."

"Listen," Edison added, "Here's 18 cents, I need the bills."

"Uh..., there's no key on the register for this. Your change is $ 1.82... here."

Edison just shook his head. He paused, looking at the change, blinked and just tossed the change into his pocket.

A moment later, he returned with the bad news.

"Uh... sorry sir, but we seem to be out of Butterfinger crunch. Would you like another mix-in.?"

"Actually no, I really only want the Butterfinger Blizzard."

"But we don't have it, sir."

"Listen, see those Butterfinger candy bars over there?"

"Yeah...?"

"Why don't you take one of those bars, break it into the mixer machine... after you unwrap it... with some vanilla ice cream and pour it all into a small cup and mix it all up?"

"Can I do that?"

"Live large, give it a shot."

"OK, man..."

"Submitted for your approval, the future lies right up ahead... the Twilight Zone." Mimicked Kate in a female version of Rod Serling. Edison chuckled, but he just had to have his Butterfinger Blizzard.

They then stopped at the local supermarket. Edison wanted to get a quart of milk and relying on the old standard that a glass of warm milk would help him get to sleep and act as a non-specific antidote against the cumulative impact of the two compound dosages he ingested earlier. He had a curiously strong yen for chocolate milk... hot cocoa actually... with the miniature marshmallows.

"Got to have hot chocolate with marshmallows tonight." He informed Kate as they got out of the car and headed through the automatic doors.

"The miniature ones, right?" Kate teased.

"Yeah, but why would you say that?"

"You just look like the miniature marshmallow type of guy. Comfort food, always has the same effect, of course it varies depending on the nature of the stress, like the pineapple, peanut butter and Ritz crackers after that big fight with Mel last winter?"

"All right smarty pants, I'm also going to get some applesauce for the Ritz crackers tonight, so what do you make of that, eh?"

"What's with this 'eh' thing, are you going Canadian on me?"

"Eh, don't want to deal with the applesauce, eh?" he taunted playfully.

"Too easy, your birthday party."

"Geez, am I that exposed... I feel almost violated!"

"Butterfinger." She deadpanned. You've got Butterfinger somewhere in your past.

Edison got it, but didn't say a word. His face became flush. He couldn't look at Kate immediately. Good thing, her face became flush, too.

[MEANWHILE]

The computer screen in the darkened room slowly scrolled the following items:

Dole Crushed Pineapple 32 oz	.89*
Motts Applesauce 30 oz	.82*
Ritz Crackers	2.79*
Big D Chocolate Milk 1 qt	1.33
Butterfinger 2 oz	.99###
Ben and Jerry's Fudge Swirl 1 pint	2.69
Thomas English Muffin 6 pack	1.72
Circus Miniature Marshmallows	.94

"Yep, something's going on here, something big." Uttered the operator in a sing-songy voice.

The operator picked up a cell phone and pressed a speed dial button, paused a moment. "Is everything status quo?"

"OK, then, I'll relieve you in an hour. You can reach me on the cell if the old guy makes another move for the baby. You're sure no one else is staking the place out? OK, you know the drill, then."

* * *

Kate insisted on coming into the condo with Edison, just to make sure he would be OK and to say hello to Mel, in case she was there. They found a note from Mel that she was staying at her cousin's with a sarcastic justification wondering "have you found that monster yet? Don't even think of calling until you do."

Edison put the perishables in the frig.

"I'm going to make a snack and go to bed... stressful day." He confessed to Kate.

As she was about to leave, she began fighting with herself on how to say good night to Edison. In a somewhat awkward motion, she made a 'V' with her right thumb and index finger and grabbed his chin and looked him firmly in the eyes.

"You call me if anything happens or you need me, understand?" … and before Edison could respond, she put her arms around him and gave him a tight hug, stretching up on her toes so make sure her cheek met his. She quickly turned around and left without making eye contact or giving Edison any opportunity to respond.

Edison settled down in bed sipping an oversized cup filled with hot chocolate, capped off with miniature marshmallows. He was too drained and was empty not having little Evan Michael around to even read a magazine and even too tired to pick up the remote to turn on the news. He propped the pillows behind his back and finished the hot chocolate. It calmed him down. "Kate was right." He thought to himself. He tried thinking about how he might vary the dosage for tomorrow, but he was unable to even connect two thoughts together and the futile attempt brought him to the point of dozing off.

All of a sudden, just as he faded into semi-consciousness, Edison began to experience fear... darkness... a light at the end of a tunnel... pressure... wet... yuck...fear... tightness... fear... the light is getting closer... is this one of those near death experiences?... no, being drawn to the light, leaving the darkness, wet... more light... more light... release... I'm into the open...wow... exhilaration... I'm not stuck anymore... freedom... fear... what is this ... fear...ouch... crying... hunger... fear... aloneness... fear... anger, frustration, anger, fuzzy visions... movement... sparkles, no, holes, like holes in a shirt eaten by moths... scratchy images, fuzzy, of faces, food, yeah, plates of food, hot open-faced turkey sandwiches, cole slaw, scoop of ice cream, no mashed potatoes, smothered in gravy... looks sorta like a diner, an old style diner... lots of people around, dishes clanging, chattering din... silence all of a sudden... anger... faces staring at me, anger... fear?...real plates, not that Styrofoam stuff... retro décor, weird, like an old 30's Bogart movie, but no Bogie. Hunger pangs... "You don't belong here, boy... outta here before I call the cops." Anger. A clenching fist... A door, a glass door, wow... old cars... a streetcar???, where in the hell did that come from? A reddish and beige streetcar, gold lettering on the side, definitely not San Francisco, though, not a cable car... Wylie Avenue street sign..."ding-ding"... anger... tension... anxiety... lust... anxiety... darkness... nothing... no images at all... blank... anxiety... lust... heavy breathing... lust... hot... squeezing... hot... lust...lust... lust...wait a minute... an image of a face, the eyes, Edison somehow recognized the eyes...

And just as quickly... the images just evaporated.

"Whew, what a dream." Edison immediately thought to himself as he scrambled to find a notepad to write down every detail before he forgot anything. He felt half soiled, half intrigued because he realized just whose eyes he had seen in his image and he realized the possible impact of the events surrounding that image. It was the disgusting image you get when you get to be old enough to first realize that your parents actually have sex together.

As was always the case, he prided himself on the logical and rational manner in which he evaluated his dreams by comparing his experiences during the previous day and drawing a connection with the dream with this current state of mind and what he had experienced during the day. He was straining to identify the connection with the images he had just dreamt. They had a certain early Picassoesqueness to them, they were a bit surreal, yet possessed almost a movie like reality/produced effect. The weird part is that most every face was black, except hers.

For several minutes, Edison struggled to make a connection with the dream he just had, but he just couldn't. "There's got to be a connection here, I must have seen a glimpse of an old movie on a TV in a store or something, didn't I? No... boy, I didn't have a hot turkey sandwich, can't remember seeing one either... wow, this is weird."

No... couldn't be... there's got to be something to tie this to what I did today...could it? No... Well, you can't totally foreclose it either, if I'm going to be scientific about this... Could it... but let's just say for arguments sake, if it was... if so, is it mom or dad, their parents. How would I be able to tell the difference? Why those images? When? Who? Nah, it seemed to real, it had to be a dream, my dream... had to come from somewhere though...But what if...

Edison knew he was on the right track... at least he wanted to believe he was... but he didn't quite know why, he certainly didn't really know how, all types of rationalizations were running through his head. He looked at the clock, and dialed his mother, even though it was very late.

"Mom... it's Ed. Yeah, I know it's late.... I'm sorry you were already asleep. Well, I know this may be weird, but I need to know your blood type. Yes I'm OK, I don't need a blood transfusion. No, it's really important it's just something I need... Please, I wouldn't be asking now if it weren't... O positive, you're sure?... Thanks... no everything is just fine, I'll fill you in later, try to go back to sleep. No, I haven't heard anything. You know I'll let you know as soon as I hear anything.... OK, OK, I'll let you know even if I don't hear anything... Well actually, there's one more thing... Did my father ever get really, really angry in a diner?... with a lot of black customers eating there? Mother, are you there?... Mother?... Mother?... It's just a question, it doesn't mean anything? Really... I was just curious, that's all, nothing more... Yeah, I'll see you tomorrow. Night."

"That must be it. I definitely hit a nerve. Well, I'm B+, so that means that my father had to be B+ too if mom is O+. It's the only explanation... Thankfully my father and I have the same blood type, should make things easier. Don't fight it, just go with it... you got lucky, don't look a gift horse..." Must have something to do with the dosage amount or the time factor or the content factor or maybe... this is getting out of hand, let's stick with what we have... let's see... I took two 20 micrograms of the compound, about fort-five minutes apart, after three hours or so... oh my god, the milk... chocolate... milk...could we be talking the functional catalyst here? Whoa, that's gotta be it... and I've got to be in a near subconscious state of meditation or being half asleep... serotonin, tryptophan? Hmmm, might have to make an early Thanksgiving meal here, turkey?"

Edison picked up the phone and called Kate.
Kate answered before Edison even heard it ring.
"Are you OK?"
"Yes, I'm OK... really... better than OK actually... you won't believe what happened ... yeah, that's a good idea. I'll put on a pot of coffee... OK, then... hot chocolate it is... yes, there are plenty of marshmallows left... I'll leave the door open."

Edison thought to himself. "Now, the sixty-four thousand dollar question... how can I control the chronology?

CHAPTER 31

Hocus Focus

The room was filled with nervous anticipation as though waiting to meet a celebrity after Edison detailed his breakthrough the previous night. All the stools were huddled in a tight circle when Edison began to detail the procedures for the next protocol.

"I'm going to use the hybrid compound at 22.5 micrograms with 2 oz of banana, all washed down by 6 oz of hot chocolate." "If it takes further dosages, I'll need to go on a diet… but…" Edison quipped. "Fortunately, I'll be doing this on an empty stomach. The only variation will be to induce a semi-conscious state I experienced with sleeping by inducing that state through hypnosis. I'm glad that Dave is experienced in past life regression hypnosis. I'm also hoping that under the guidance of hypnosis, we might better be able to manage the chronology of the impressions.

After reviewing in my own mind what happened last night, I'm convinced that the images I experienced were among the highest and most recent levels of emotional memories, which may have caused them to attach first in relation to all the other experiences. That is why I am increasing the single dosage, in order to penetrate the less emotional experiences and with any luck, they will be sequential and not appear to be random access. Is everyone ready?"

"Will you be able to recount everything verbally as you experience the images, if you're under hypnosis?"

"I'll make that suggestion to him. He should be free to fully relay any impressions he is experiencing as hypnosis is really not much more that a subconscious state where he is aware of everything."

"Anything else?"

"No."

"OK, then, let's go, times a wasting." Edison offered.

Edison took the banana chunk, chewed the entire thing at once. The crystals of the compound made for a gritty additive and tasted as though he were eating sand in the banana. He was actually happy to wash down the whole thing with the hot chocolate. At that moment, he realized that he didn't have the marshmallows in the hot chocolate like the night before, but he quickly put that out of his mind being confident that it was the cocoa and not the sucrose in the marshmallows that more than likely acted as the catalyst.

Edison then relaxed in the recliner, while Dave began to put him under. Given the monotone of Dave's voice, it would have been easy to put the entire group to sleep, if it were not for the anticipation shown in the eyes of the group.

"If he doesn't get any results from this, at least he can make him cluck like a chicken later." Dave whispered.

"That's so banal. Julie responded. "I'd prefer a duck."

The lights were dimmed to near darkness.

"Edison, can you hear me?"

"Yes."

"Good. In a few moments you are going to begin experiencing a peaceful.. restful state. What I would like for you to do is to describe whatever images to the best of your ability, in as much detail as you can, is that clear?"

"Yes."

"This sounds like a past life regression." Julie whispered.

"Good. I want you to imagine getting into an elevator and push the button for the basement. Let me know when the door opens."

"OK, I'm there."

"Now it's dark, but in a moment, I'll have you open a door at the end of the hallway and let me know what you see. After you describe an image, I may ask you questions about it and ask to you go ahead to see what else you're seeing, OK.

"OK."

"Relax now and go ahead and open that door and let me know when you begin to see anything."

After a couple seconds, Edison began:

"I feel like I'm floating in air, in an out, I see a cloud, a mist, like I'm going through a cloud, like flying a plane, feet first... and now...now... whoa... I'm walking down the street... Beauty Academy... dark... must be night... everyone's black... smoke... yuccch... smokey bar....bar... tables, stools... ugh filthy floor... stale beer... bottles, brown beer bottles, Iron City... Duquesne... brown bottles... booze... darkness... everything is brownish... like those old photos used in Butch Cassidy and the Sundance Kid movie... some tints, but brown, scratchy like an old movie, not black and white though, brown hues... a piano... black and white keys... terror... Will I be able to play without screwing up?... If I screw up will they pay me? ... Hunger..., I could sure eat... Just a few Ritz crackers... I'm playing... this is good... why are my hands dark..., I can feel these ivories, I'm part of this thing... what was I worrying about... anxiety... I don't want to do this... I'm hungry... no choice... gotta do it... shit... this ain't right...

Whew... a dial... this is one big mother safe... how the hell did they get this on a train?... hurry... OK... hurry... If we get caught... all right, feel the dial... you know you can do this... why did they have to knock that guard out?... 45... yea... two times right now... hurry... ah... yeah... yeah... 88, nah, too easy for a player... yeah... 88, OK now... left again... feel it... feel it... slow... slow now... 30? Damn I'm good... "I got it!"... I can't believe I did this, damn...

"That's why we call you 'Fingers, if you weren't so damn ugly I'd kiss you." Came a male voice to the right.

There he is... brown hair, nice suit... weird... like some speakeasy suit... weird... shifty eyes, craggy face... whoa, don't point that gun at me, man... whoa, look at all them gold coins, there must be hundreds... thousands of them...

"Let's get out of here... JUMP!" he yelled.

Jump shit, I ain't jumpin... man that tressle must be at least 10-15 feet...

"Here comes the train dick... JUMP YOU MOTHA FUCK...!"...

"ooooooooohh SHIT.... My stomach feels like it's being sucked up into my throat... bam! Jesus be, I jumped... Am I OK, I'm not dead at least, any broken bones... no... OK... never again...

(Hey, you know you never die from jumping in a dream... Edison thought to himself.)

"Get up you fuck...Get your bones outta here... get to the car... the kid's waitin!"

Running, running, running, outta breath, shit I ain't no Jim Thorpe... running... damn, there's a cop... look cool... don't look at him... don't look away... hold your breath... he's going to cuff me for sure... why do they always stop me...mad... anger...whoa... there he goes, running toward the train... I'm never going to do this again no matter what... this ain't worth it... nothin's worth this... where the fuck is the car... where's Elam? There he is, shit he was supposed to be over there... damn, why won't this door open... geez, this kid doesn't even shave yet...he musta just got his license... he's still one mean looking kid...

"What the fuck's wrong with you kid... the cops are after us and your throwing trash out the window... are you fucking crazy... get us the fuck outta here."

Oh shit here come the cops... hurry up... get us outta here... cut down the alley... there's another alley down to the right... it dumps out on .... Yeah, just cut across the Market, go to the back it goes to ...

"Shut up you old shit..." I can out drive you with my eyes closed and one arm tied behind my back!" he yelled... Harry... the Kid, shit why do we have a kid doin this?

"We lost him... good job kid... !" he whooped... X

Who's the dame... ? Red lip stick, what is this the McGuire Sisters?...When do I get my share?... You better not jake me off.

You can't use these coins, they gotta be fenced, too new.

You better not jake me off.

I ain't goin to jake you off Eddie, your'e too ugly.. and besides, I need you... you son of a bitch... we did it... we did it... Jesus be, we did it....! We did it... we did it... we did it..............

Edison took a deep breath and sighed. The compound was wearing off. Everyone stood around mesmerized, frozen. Was this some type of psycho hallucination... some past life regression...could it really be memories from Edison's father?...

Later, when Edison listened to the tape with Will, years of research and the gut feel of vindication welled up. He knew these visions were consistent with his mother's story. It was too real to be some dream-like extrapolation from that story, it was too real, the beer bottles, the street sign, the beauty academy, the Bar, the piano, the train... the gold coins... the gold coins... that's what the old guy must be after... the gold coins... Christ remember... what year was the mint on the coins, I saw them when the safe was opened... what year, think... remember... 19... 19... 193.....1930, 1932, 1933! Yeah. Looked like the lady in the nightgown on the front and the flying eagle on the back...they were big, like silver dollars... UNITED STATE OF AMERICA...TWENTY DOLLARS...gotta get a coin book, forgot where I put the other one back home... yeah, 1930 something... the numbers were rounded, 3,0,2, not 1,7 or 4.

Will started doing a search on the internet... "Iron City and Duquesne, that sounds like Pittsburgh, PA, Edison... and Wylie Ave, there's a Wylie Avenue in Pittsburgh, too, that's probably what you saw." "Says here Wylie Avenue is in the Hill District, must be the Beacon Hill section of Pittsburgh, probably." Will offered.

*   *   *

Beep...Beep...

The computer screen awoke from the energy saver sleep mode.

"What do we have here."

Beep... Beep...

Authorization for MasterCard 4530 3333 ....

Edison A. Barr

Ben's Booksellers
Springfield, MA
15280

$ 6.99   Blackbook price guide to US Coins

.35   MA Sales Tax

$ 7.34   Total Sale

"YES!" "A coin book. The son of a bitch must've found the coins! The son of a bitch found the fuckin coins!" YES!... Pop... were gonna do this, Pop... it's gonna happen... I can't believe it.... Its gonna happen, I can taste it, now! Forty years of sweat, Pop, we're gonna do it. I promised you on your grave, we're gonna do it and we are!" You were right all along, the kid knew where the coins were. He was the key...

"Oh man, let see, even if only a 1000 coins at even $ 15,000 apiece is $ 15 mil at 10%.... Shit... One million five hundred thousand finder's fee... even after taxes, that's got to be at least one mil net. Oh Pop, I'll get Ma a new house, a new car, don't worry Pop, I'll take care of her, don't you worry... Or how about all 15 mil... ? and no taxes... no don't even think about that, the reward money is... sorry Pop, just a thought... sorry I didn't really mean it... sorry."

* * *

Edison felt like he was on a scavenger hunt as he opened the guide book. "What did those coins look like... let's see, gold coins.. twenty dollars...Morgan Heads... no...Liberty Heads... no...whoa, this looks close... Standing Liberty... could be, but these are all 190.... Something...Liberty Standing St. Gaudens, now this looks close, real close...1908...1913...1925...1930S, 1931, no, 1931D, no... 1932 and 1933. This has gotta be it.

"How much are they worth already?" Will asked really antsy.

"You're not going to believe this, Will... assuming these coins are in uncirculated condition, which has to be the case, each one.... Depending on the year, well they average... like $ 25,000 each!"

"Yo... and just how many of these did you envision here?"

"God, the box was maybe two feet long, nine to ten inches high and maybe nine or ten inches deep. And it was filled... at least back then...

"Well, let's see, at twenty coins a roll, stacked two high, three rolls across times maybe 10 rolls long, we're talking like... could be 1,200 or more coins. Do the math... 1,200 coins at $15,000 each looks like $ 18 Million bucks... and dare I say... tax free if they're found!?"

"Well, I guess that's what the old guy is after, eh?

"And he's been looking for these since the 60's?"

"More than likely."

"I wouldn't recommend getting in his way. He's like a bull in a china shop, but with a five decade running start. What are you going to do?"

"Like I really have a choice. You say it sounded like I saw things in Pittsburgh?"

"Well, unless you can get a Duquesne or Iron City Beer in Springfield... and there is a Wylie Avenue in Pittsburgh, so..."

"Well, I guess I'm going to Pittsburgh. Wonder if my mother knows anything about this?"

Kate instinctively responded, "Well, you can't go by yourself, you'll need some help. Will, you available?"

"I can't take time off of work right now, we're just installing a whole new hardware sub-system at work."

"That settles it. My brother is gonna kill me, but I'm going to go with you. We have to take off two weeks of vacation time anyway since Mel just had the baby, so I've got the time. Let's do it."

"You sure?" Edison asked. He has been very guarded about being around other women without Mel being there, but strangely, he felt comfortable with her offer, as being someone he could trust sharing his ideas with, as the next best thing if Will wasn't available.

"Positive. I've never been to Pittsburgh and besides, what are we talking about, a day or two, no sweat."

[MEANWHILE]

Beep... Beep...

The computer screen awoke from the energy saver sleep mode.

"What do we have here."

Beep... Beep...

Authorization for MasterCard 4530 3333 ....
Edison A. Barr

US Airways
RT BDL/PIT............$ 215.00
RT BDL/PIT..............215.00

Total.........................430.00
Total charge...............430.00
Amount Due.................0.00

"PIT... Pittsburgh?... can't be Pittsfield..."
The operator immediately logged onto ORBITZ and checked fares for immediate departure for BDL-PIT.
"That's it..." as he clicked on the "Purchase this Fare" button. "Wonder who's he going with?"

Moments later.

Beep... Beep...
Authorization for MasterCard 4530 3333 ....
Edison A. Barr

Priceline.com

Full Size
Thrifty Rent a Car.......$ 129.00
Service Charge..................7.00

Total Charge..................136.00
Amount Due:....................0.00

Edison and Kate drove to the airport stopping at the off-site parking facility and took the mini bus to the air terminal A for US Airways. They only had one carry-on and they shared a check in overnighter, which they checked in at the curb with the skycap.

Tom Dugan followed them in his official detective's car, a Mercury Grand Marquis, dark brown with standard hubcaps and the small antenna sprouting over the trunk. For an unmarked car, hardly anyone would mistake this for anything but an unmarked police car.

Hacksaw was following both groups in his metallic blue 1976 Caddy. When he saw them dropped off at the US Air Terminal at Bradley Airport, he illegally left his car at the drop off circle and watched as they checked in for the 2:33 nonstop flight to Pittsburgh (PIT), with continuing service to Nashville (BNA).

Hack confirmed the destination was PIT from the baggage tag on the overnighter.

"Pittsburgh, yeah, that's where Artie boy was from alright. That's a ten hour drive, better get fueled up and on the road." Harry Elam never flew... and was not about to start now. He didn't trust anything he couldn't handle himself. Totally old school.

CHAPTER 32

An Interview with Miss Louise

"I think we're looking for Centre Avenue, where are we now?" Kate asked.

"Ah, we.. are.. on… just a minute… 6th Avenue… and… Smithfield." Edison responded.

"OK, if we keep going straight, it should curve around and we should hit Centre Ave, then hang a left." Kate claimed while examining the road map provided by the rental company.

"So what are we looking for once we get there?"

"I don't really know, we'll have to play it by ear. Maybe something will look familiar from the sessions."

As they crossed onto Centre Avenue, Kate exclaimed, "Oh my god…!"

"Whaaat?"

"A huge… UFO has landed right around the corner!"

"Get serious."

"Edison, I am, I'm not joking around!"

"Oh geez, that's not a UFO."

"If there ever was a flying saucer, that's it… and if that's not a UFO, then what is it?"

"That's the Igloo… the Civic Arena… its where the Pittsburgh Penguins play… they're a NHL hockey team… you know… Mario Lemeiux… Stanley Cup? "

"You mean that's like the Garden… the Bruins?

"Well, it looks like it's now the… Mellon Arena, another corporate sponsorship… another sports venue bites the dust. The '84 Olympics… that's where it all got started, sell your soul to the corporate store for naming rights to the arena."

"My god, it looks like it should be at Disney's Futureworld.

"Actually, it's a bit long in the tooth, they were talking about building a new one."

When they saw got onto Centre Avenue they saw Wylie Avenue.

"Well, there's Wylie Avenue, I wonder if it's the same one I saw."

As they paused at the corner of Centre and Wylie Avenues, they looked at each other with surprise and disappointment. They both had this impression that the Hill District would be the Pittsburgh equivalent of the upscale Beacon Hill area of Boston. They both were experiencing the clear lack of quality, where reality turns out to be less than the expectation, in this case, much less. The Hill District in reality seems to be an economically depressed area. They both were experiencing the effect of the deer in the headlight syndrome, where any plans they may have had were immediately dashed.

"Now what?" Kate asked as though the wind was knocked out of her.

"Well, let's take a ride up the hill and see what happens. Maybe this place was the upscale area way back then."

"I can't believe this is what you saw… you know, there could be a Wylie Avenue in other cities."

"Come on, I know my mother and father spent time in Pittsburgh, before they got married. This must be it… besides, we were talking decades ago. Anything could've happened since then."

"If you insist."

"Not much going on here, but this place feels eerily familiar, but that's probably just my wishful thinking."

"Edison, there's nothing here." Kate offered after driving the length of Wylie Avenue.

"Well, let's go back... do you see anything remotely like a beauty salon, an old diner type restaurant, a bar, anything?"

"Well, that church over there looks like it's still going on. It might be open."

"You know, that's not a bad idea, maybe an old pastor or parishioner might be able to give us a clue."

"Pull right over there, you can park."

*   *   *

As they got out of the car and stretched themselves a bit and headed into the church, Tom, driving a dark blue Buick Regal pulled up and parked a half a block down the Avenue on the other side. He was wearing sunglasses and just sat in the car as though this was nothing new... and it wasn't... just another stakeout, albeit in Pittsburgh rather than Springfield, and he's following his little sister.

*   *   *

"Hello, I'm father Larry... can I help you?"

"Good afternoon... yes... this might sound a bit on the unusual side, but I'm looking for someone."

"And who might that be... someone in the church?"

"Well, that's where it gets unusual, I don't really know whom I'm looking for."

"Well, that is an unusual request, but that's OK with me, I love a good mystery, but you've got to give me a clue... are you with the police?"

"Oh geez no... I'm just doing some research for a book I'm writing and I guess I'm looking for someone who might have known someone who might have lived here back in the 30's and 40's."

"Aha... and who might have lived here back in the 30's and 40's?

"I believe his name was Eddie Clark, he might have been a musician... a piano player."

"Well, that's a real possibility... Wylie Avenue had the best jazz between Chicago and New York back in those days, just a little before my time, though, he winked."

"Mine too."

"You know, we had some researchers up here a while ago that were asking around for that Ken Burns' Jazz documentary on PBS. You with them

"No, this is a private effort."

"Jazz?"

"Well it's certainly part of the story."

"Well, I'm thinking... you know, Miss Louise has lived here all her life... I'm wondering if she might be able to help you out."

"Great, where can we find her."

"Actually she came to mind since she's here right now in the Senior Activity Room... and if she can't help, there might be someone else here today who might be helpful. Follow me, if you would."

"Miss Louise, I'd like you to meet... ?"

"Oh, hi, I'm Edison Barr and this is my friend Kate Dugan."

"Pleasure to make your acquaintance, young man, and you too young lady. You two married?"

"No ma'am. Just good friends."

"Shame. You two make a nice young couple."

"Miss Louise, they were wondering if you might have some recollection of a musician that might have played some of the clubs around here back in the 30's and 40's?"

"Well don't just stand there, c'mon over here and let's talk. Thank you father, we'll take it from here. I have fond memories back then. Wylie Avenue was the crossroads to the world back then. My oh my, you better not get me started..." Miss Louise started with widened eyes.

No one had engaged her in a trip down memory lane for quite some time and she was primed.

"Well, I don't even know if he lived here back then, but I'm trying to find out about a piano player by the name of Edward Clark... Edward A. Clark."

"Woa'ee... now there's a name I haven't thought about in ages... you mean 'ol Fingers?...Artie 'Fingers' Clark... ha, ha ha." She cackled.

"Ah... could be, ma'am."

"Now that was some boy, ooeee, could I tell you stories about that boy.

Edison and Kate sunk into the burnt red vinyl sofa knowing that they may have just hit the mother lode.

Edison's eyes widened as fast as initial inflation just after the big bang, and his heart was racing and he could feel his blood pressure increasing... finally... stories about his father, unbelievable after all this time... thinking, "Why didn't I do this before now?"

"You know, I never believed that boy's name was Clark though. We always said he made that up."

"Why is that?

"Y'know that boy... you never saw that boy 'lest he were eatin a candy bar... always a Clark bar. We always said, he was keeping the Clark bar factory downtown (pronounce, dahntahn in Pittsburghese) in business single handedly."

"Clark bar?"

"Sure, child, y'know, peanut butter crunch with a chocolate coating... sorta like a Butterfinger. You're not from around here are you? He always joked that he was the part owner of the Clark bar factory, but we all knew that couldn't be. Now how do you know Fingers, is he still alive?"

Kate shot Edison a long look. Nothing had to be said. Although she couldn't be sure, she felt as though Edison was thinking the same thing. Butterfinger.

"Actually no, I've been told he died back in the 60's and we're from Massachusetts." Edison replied.

"Too cold up there for my old bones, do you know what happened?"

"Not really, that's what I'm trying to figure out."

Out of nowhere, she asked, "Are you the one?" Miss Louise piped up right out of left field.

"I'm not sure what you mean, ma'am. Edison replied.

Miss Louise purposefully changed the direction of the conversation.

"Anyway, you know that boy would always be hangin out in front of the La Salle... that was a beauty academy back then... waiting for aallll the pretty girls to come out. Hee, hee, he would pick his girl for the day and give her a Clark bar to go to Nesbit's Pie Shop for a bowl of vanilla ice cream... and you know what he'd do then?" "He'd go and smash up that Clark bar into little pieces right into the ice cream and smush it all together until it was one big smushy mess... but whoa'ee, was that good... y'know, I haven't had one of those is years!" "My lord..." she smiled in fond remembrance. And if he really liked you, he'd get a piece of their sweet potato pie, too.

Kate again shot Edison a look that even lasted a moment longer. Butterfinger Bizzard! For Edison, these revelations not only gave him a much needed insight into his father after all these years, but also eerily ratified his DNA research, and to some degree, and Kate's lab rat work.

"Sounds like you were one of his dates." Kate jumped in.

"Oh, child..." Miss Louise said as she became visibly embarrassed. We was just kids back then, hee, hee."

Edison was going limp all over. He had heard more about his father in these few minutes than from his mother in his entire lifetime.

"Do you know how he got his nickname 'Fingers'? Edison asked.

"Child, that boy had fingers on him that... well, that boy should've been a brain surgeon." Miss Louise capped her mouth with her left hand as she remembered an intimate moment from a life, long, long ago. "Y'know, he was one of the best piano players that every went through Wylie Avenue, and that includes Earl Hynes and Billy Strayhorn. But, lord he just wouldn't listen to anyone about how to play... if he couldn't play his way, then he wasn't gonna play for anyone, no matter what, mind you. If that boy had just listened to Earl or Billy, he coulda been a real star. What a shame... that boy sure had talent. You know he could feel anything with those fingers of his... I remember that old Gus from Crawford's would give him 50 cents to tell him who was lying and who was telling the truth. Fingers... all he had to do is to touch your face when you were asked a question and he could tell if you were lyin or telling the truth! Can ya believe that?!? That boy was like a living lie detector machine. He could tell you what kind of wood it was, what kind of material it was, just by touchin it, with his eyes closed shut, mind you... You know they say you get better senses when you go blind, kinda to compensate."

"Are you saying Eddie was blind?"

"No, child, haha, ha..., she cackled. His momma was blind... he musta gotten it from her, the touch, you know... And that's what got him into trouble, too."

"Trouble?" Edison asked somewhat surprised.

"Now don't misunderstand me, now, but you have to remember back then, times were real tough. It was still the depression back then and you had to do what you had to do to get by. Now when someone needed to get into something, Fingers was the one they called.

I mean, even if someone forgot the numbers to get into their safe, well, Fingers could dial up those numbers faster than they could when they remembered the numbers. He could open just about any lock that had a key to it, I mean there wasn't a lock or safe that Fingers couldn't get into with just those fingers of his..." Miss Louise paused again as she was reliving yet another pleasant moment from the past.

"Now, he never hurt no one, mind you. He would never hurt no one. He had a real good heart. He just couldn't say no when someone needed to get into something. You know, child, you have his eyes. Your sure you're not from around here?" She inquired.

"Are you suggesting he might have done something illegal?"

"Now I'm not goin to start anything here, but there were stories, you know, that's all I can say."

"Can you remember when that was...?

"Oooh, that must have been sometime after the crash... but before the war, maybe in the early 30's or so, maybe. He was into something with that Weiss boy, now there was one bad apple.

"You wouldn't remember what he looked like would you?"

"That boy had a face, mean... looked like he had the pox as a child, that boy was mean... and uuuuggggly, hehee", she cackled.

"You know, I can remember back then better than what I did this morning!" She laughed. "And you know, that's when I saw that little white girl who was sweet for him, hanging around here. You know, he was real partial to that girl, too. I wonder whatever happened to her."

"Do you remember her name?"

"Who, Weiss or Fingers?"

"Fingers."

"Well, she was learning beauty at the La Salle with all the other girls. But she would always go down to the Stanley, the Celebrity Bar or to Crawfords Grill to hear Fingers play. She was real fond of him and his music and all. I remember she was real mad when they wouldn't let her join the Ducks with the rest of us."

"The Ducks?"

"Oh, that was a social club for all us girls, you know, like the Frogs were for the boys." "We'd have dances, meetings, pageants and things. She couldn't understand why she couldn't join. I felt sorry for her, but she was getting to understand what it was like, you know, segregation and all that colored / white thing goin on back then. She just didn't fit in. Fingers was real mad, too. Dorothy... yeah oh my... that was her name."

"You mean Fingers was...." Kate stopped herself short when she realized the situation, half in shock. Edison had already half realized his father's racial background from piecing together the images he saw during his sessions and the black hands playing the piano in the picture hanging in his mother's den... and maybe why Dorothy was acting so weird around Will at the hospital when Evan was born and why she seemed embarrassed to discuss anything about the past with him. Again, he couldn't get the image of his young mothers face out of his mind from his first session. It must have been the apex of his father's emotional experiences to pop out first. That made him feel warm all over... his father and mother really loved each other, despite the obvious age and racial hurdles.

Kate couldn't help but stand up, running her fingers through her hair above and across the sides of her head, tugging on the roots, slowly shaking at the revelation. She couldn't get the thought out of her mind and why she didn't figure it out earlier.

Kate just withdrew and thought, "What is Mel going to do... what the hell is Mel going to do. Does Edison realize that Melissa has a real racial bias to her? Kate had heard it many times, including snide remarks about Edison's best friend, Will. No way she knows this." Kate lost the conversation and began realizing a lot of things that had gone unexplained about Edison in the past which now were falling into place like the final cards in the Solitaire game in Windows. Kate then returned to the conversation as Miss Louise continued...

"You know, there were days Fingers would just go down to La Salle's and let all the girls just rub his head, all day sometimes. He just loved having his head rubbed! He would just let them practice on him so they could do boy's hair just as easy as girl's hair, too."

"Would you remember where Weiss was from?"

"I do believe that boy came from under a rock and I hope that's where he went back to. He was a bad one. Could never see what Fingers was doin with him... nothing good, to be sure."

"And who was Weiss with?

"You mean that Asian girl?"

"You mean Chinese?"

"No... she was Hawaiian I do believe. She just loved pineapple... even got Fingers into eating pineapple... Clark bars and pineapple with peanut butter on Ritz crackers, lord I don't know how that boy survived eatin like that all the time."

"You wouldn't remember where in Hawaii she was from, now would you?

"Child, all I can remember is something like, my lord, you know those Hawaiian names are sounding alike, like... hoity hoity... or something like that."

"Are you the one?" Miss Louise asked, not realizing she had already asked earlier.

"I honestly don't know what you're talking about, ma'am, Edison replied.

"I almost forgot the most important thing." Miss Louise pondered to herself. "I sure didn't think so much time would pass, but, you know, I like your eyes, child you have familiar eyes."

"Thank you." Edison came back.

"Well, I don't know what this all means, but Fingers told me before he disappeared that if anyone should come looking for him, cepting Lt. Bush, the policeman, mind you, that I should tell them something for Fingers."

"What's that?", Kate asked.

"Well, back then the numbers writers, you know, the numbers... well anyway, they had this secret code for their numbers... and Fingers told me to tell anyone who might be comin around askin about him what the secret code was. I guess telling you after all these years can't do no one any harm, I mean they haven't done that in years. Anyway, child, Fingers told me to tell, so I'm going to tell... there was this secret code, ROOT NAILS they used to hide all their numbers on the slips, you know?

"ROOT NAILS?" Edison asked intently.

"That's right ROOT NAILS. I don't know what it means, but the secret code was ROOT NAILS. Each letter means a number, like one through ten or something like that."

"But how can you have two of the same letters, then?" Asked Edison in his best researcher tone.

"I don't know, child, that was the secret code they used and that's what Fingers told me to tell anyone who came looking for him, so that's all I know. Fingers said you'd know what it meant. Well, child, I've got to be tending to my friends, it's getting close to supper time. You know, I've really enjoyed this." Miss Louise cackled and laughing.

"Miss Louise, I can't tell you how glad I am to have stopped by and met you. It's such a pleasure to meet someone with your experiences to share."

"My pleasure, child, now are the two of you getting married?"

"No, ma'am, we're not."

"Well, what in the world are you waiting for, child, the streetcar's a coming and you'd better hop on it. If there are two people who look like they should be married, and makin a family, you two are the ones."

Edison could only think about Evan and didn't put much credence into Miss Louise's observation.

Kate, however, felt like she had just read a horoscope that validated her feelings of the past several months. She could see it didn't faze Edison, but if Miss Louise saw it, then that's all she needed to finally act on her feelings.

As Kate and Edison said their goodbyes to Miss Louise and began to leave, Kate asked Father Larry, who was strolling down the hallway,

"Father Larry, thank you so much for introducing us to Miss Louise."

"My pleasure, I hope you all had a pleasant conversation."

"We most certainly did, father." Edison said.

"By the way, do you know of a good place to grab a sandwich or something?"

"Well, if you're from out of town and want to meet people your own age, I'd recommend going down to the Strip District, off of Penn Avenue and go to Primanti's. They got the world's best sandwiches."

"Thanks, again Father, for the introduction and the restaurant recommendation."

"Again, my pleasure, and may your quest in life find happiness and peace be with you, both."

*   *   *

Tom slinked down into his seat when Edison and Kate drove by. He certainly didn't want his sister to know he was there.

LATER IN HIS ROOM...

On Tom's computer screen...

Pittsburgh.com... Restaurants...CLICK... Best 'Burgh Bites...CLICK... Pizza... CLICK...

Vincent's Pizza Park   Forest Hills
Mineo's Squirrel Hill... CLICK...

MAP/DIRECTIONS

"Mineo's... Sounds good... should do the trick..." Tom thought to himself. Pop would approve. Squirrel Hill...? Yikes..., well, I'll have to sneak away sometime tomorrow and check it out."

CHAPTER 33

Follow the Leader

The menu board at Primanti's listed all of the dozens of sandwich options available. There were dozens of people moving around this busy place. Edison was happy, because he knew any place as busy as this would have good food. Although the prices seemed a bit on the high side, $ 6.95 on average given the decor, they did not even contemplate going elsewhere. The tables were butcher-block tops with bottles of Heinz ketchup and two varieties of mustard, yellow and deli brown. A stainless steel bowl of pickles complemented the paper place mats and the napkin wrapped fork and knife. There was a long sandwich prep table behind the order register. Edison was hungry, given the emotional roller coaster he had just disembarked from and needed some red meat, so he ordered the roast beef. Kate went for the turkey.

"Anything to drink with that?" asked the college age order taker, who looked suspiciously like the sandwich guru laboring building sandwiches with the flair of the Pittsburgh Symphony maestro.

"What do you have?" inquired Edison.

"Well, the usual, Coke, Sprite, Diet Coke, Root Beer, iced tea, coffee and Blennd."

"Blennd, what's that?"

"You're not from around here are ya?"

"Is there a sign on my back?"

"Nah, it's just a local thing, un-carbonated lemon-lime-orange drink. In fact, if you want to be adventuresome, try a half and half... half iced tea and half blend, really good."

"Sold." Said Edison.

"Sign me up for a diet Coke, if you would." Kate requested.

"OK, that will be $ 17.40. We'll bring it out to our table in a couple minutes."

Edison thought that was a little steep for two sandwiches and two drinks and why would Father Larry recommend a place with these kind of prices.

Kate and Edison were quiet in the car on the way to Primanti's. Kate knew that he needed time to assimilate the information provided by Miss Louise. Edison always was a better communicator while eating, so she waited until the food was served until she began the questions.

They both chuckled when the food arrived. These were no ordinary sandwiches. They were more like meals in between two slices of fresh Italian bread, soft in the center and crusty on the edges. The thinly sliced roast beef and turkey was layered under a heap of cole slaw, tomatoes and French fries all part of the sandwich kind of smooshed together right into the sandwich. Smooshed was quickly moving into Edison's lexicon, lately.

They came wrapped in deli tissue and served in a wicker basket. This was going to be messy, but good.

Timed perfectly after Edison swallowed the first dripping bite, Kate tossed up the first question.,

"So what do you make of this ROOT NAILS thing.?

As though he were on a first date and didn't know whether to finish swallowing, take another bite or actually answer the question, he chose to put the sandwich down for two reasons, one to get a handle on how to eat this thing and second to explore the possibilities with Kate.

"Well, I know that most retail places have a code where they list the cost of whatever they're selling listed on a tag, like MONEY TALKS, that's what I use, so that if someone tries to dicker with them on price, they can figure how much of a discount to give without going below their cost, like if you go to buy a TV, refrigerator or something." "Each letter corresponds to a number, so for MONEY TALKS, there are ten letters representing 1-0, so $ 17.40 would be MA.ES, or 1,7,4,0... but ROOT NAILS has only nine letters."

"Are you thinking we should have dickered for the sandwiches."

"No, just an example. And I'm sure that they used this to encode all the numbers slips from the customers that went to the numbers writers, so the cops wouldn't know or prove anything, but for a listing of letters. What's curious is… hmmm… what to do with ROOT NAILS… it has two O's. Why would they do that, there must be some system to figure out when an O is a two or a three. Maybe they never used a 2 or a 3 for their betting slips to throw off the cops." Edison winked and smiled. "Too bad Tom isn't here, he might help us out with that one."

"Why are you looking at me like that for… just because my father was a cop and my brother is one too? Hey, police work is an honorable profession, and besides, running numbers isn't exactly like running the church bingo night."

"Hey, don't misunderstand me, the numbers are no different from the lottery. Now it's just legalized. What do you think it's all about, I mean there must've been something with numbers or something."

"Did you see anything with numbers in your sessions?"

"Nah, nothing I can remember, but given what Miss Louise was talking about, it's got to be something like the combination to an old safe or a telephone number or... whatever, but after all these years?

"An address... or the winning Megabucks for this week?"

"I think he was a piano player who broke into some safe, not a card carrying member of the psychic friends network."

"And how about that Miss Louise?"

"What a treasure!"

Kate gazed around the restaurant and out of the corner of her eye, noticed a dark blue car parked in front of the restaurant, but didn't make any conscious connection as being the car she saw out of the corner of her eye back at the church.

*   *   *

"I assume you'll want a separate room?" Edison asked Kate as they were walking into the lobby of the Days Inn.

"Really, there's no need to waste the money, I think I can trust you? I'm sure we'll be up most of the night talking, so just get double beds and a shower with lots of hot water."

"Are you sure?"

"Sure."

"OK... then why do I feel like a teenager getting a motel room for the first time. Should I use 'Smith' or something?

"Just use VISA, that oughta do it."

"One double room, for how many nights?" asked the clerk.

"One or two."

"Will you paying with a credit card?"

"Yeah, here you go."

"I'll just authorize this and leave it open until I hear from you."

"That will be fine."

"Would you like me to activate the phone for you?"

"OK, but if I need to, I'll probably use my cell phone."

"Don't worry, if you don't use it there won't be any charge for it."

"Works for me.

*   *   *

Kate spent 39 minutes in the shower, while Edison lay on the bed, reminiscing about the information he learned about his father from Miss Louise. It was sweet. All these years, not knowing anything, and now, a picture of Eddie 'Finger's' Clark was coming into focus, from his lab sessions and from Miss Louise. This was nice. The Clark bar, the pineapple, the Ritz crackers. At least he now understands his subliminal connection with Butterfinger Blizzards, the Clark bar workaround. Alternatively, he felt pangs of anger with his mother, then quickly changed thoughts after seeing that image of his mother, young and vital, in his vision.

"Nothing better than a motel shower, where you don't have to worry about using up all the hot water. My brother would always yell at me if I stayed in any longer than 10 minutes. "What the hell you doing in there Sis, Hey Sis, you're going to go down the drain, Hey Sis, you're going to melt away if you don't come out of there... oy.... Now I feel guilty for taking a long shower. I feel like one of our conditioned rats."

"Just how high is the shower nozzle? I can't stand some motels, the nozzle is about at my navel level."

"It's up there, you should be OK."

Edison came out of the shower and Kate asked, "Hey, since your father like to have his head rubbed, I'm guessing... would you like one?" Kate asked hopefully.

"I love to have my head rubbed... you'd do that for me?"

"Jackpot..." Kate thought to herself..." Sure, why not?"

"Mel hates doing it. Even in a good mood, she'll do it for a minute or so, then get distracted and walk away."

"Well, I may not be a La Salle girl, but... Come on over here and put your head in my lap and let's see how it goes."

"I owe you one..." offered Edison.

Kate began to stroke her fingers through Edison's thinning hair. She was enjoying this even beyond her own expectations. She started in the front and worked her slender fingers back and down the nape of his neck, gently squeezing and pulling on his hair this way and that.

"What's this... getting a little bald back here, Ed!" she playfully teased him.

"Does this motel provide Rogaine in the bathroom?"

"I didn't see any."

"Well, I guess you shouldn't pull too hard then..."

"I'll use my nails and scratch your scalp a little bit... to stimulate the blood flow of course..."

"Screw the Rogaine." Edison quipped, "How about Viagra?"

Even though Kate knew he wasn't making any kind of pass at her, it was still a warm feeling knowing that Edison would even quip about a sexual reference with her. "This is good." Kate thought. Edison was a bit surprised he actually make a pseudo sexual reference while his head was in a prone position in Kate's lap.

Kate continued rubbing and alternative scratching Edison's scalp. They were both enjoying it… a real sense of comfort and pure satisfaction... until Kate stopped and began to pull gently on Edison's hair around the growing bald spot on the back of his head.

"Edison?" Kate suddenly stopped and asked.

"Uh huh." Edison slowly responded as though he was lost in quiet ecstasy.

"Edison, there's something on your head."

"Yeah, I know, thinning hair, just keep rubbing."

"No, I'm serious, there's something on your head!"

Edison sat up…"Like what?"

"Dark blue… marks… dots on your head.?"

"I wasn't aware Diet Coke was hallucinogenic."

"Edison Barr, I'm serious… You have dark blue dots over the back of your head... looks like domino dots!"

She continued tugging and pulling on his hair off to the side.

"There's some more… and some more… this is weird!"

"You might want to see your ophthalmologist when we get back."

"I'm not crazy, here look in my hand mirror."

"I can't see anything."

Kate got up and pushed him towards the mirror over the credenza holding the hand mirror to reflect off of the wall mirror next to the lamp.

"Look!" said Kate as Edison adjusted the hand mirror to view the back of his scalp.

"You mean those things?"

"Yeah, those things."

"Geez, I've never seen those before… what do they look like… they don't feel like bumps or anything, oh jeez, they're just some kind of birthmark!"

"If these are birthmarks I'll rub your head until you go completely bald."

"That's a hard choice, having birthmarks or getting a lifetime head rub!"

"These aren't birthmarks!"

"OK, then, what do they look like?"

"Like… like… domino tiles, yeah, domino tiles… or dice.

"Don't tell me, there are domino dots on my head, yeah, sure!"

"Well then, you tell me… I'm getting a scissors out of my purse."

"And just what are you going to do with them… I happen to like my ears and I have no interest in looking like Van Gough."

"I'm going to cut away enough hair to see what's there."

"You're not going to cut my hair!"

"Don't sweat it… there's not that much hair to cut, if you catch my drift."

"Aw, come on… you've heard too many stories about beauty academies today."

"Sit down, this won't hurt a bit."

"Am I going to have to buy a hat tomorrow morning?"

"Just sit still, unless of course you want that Van Gough look!"

"I can't believe I'm letting you do this."

"Edison, forget the ear."

"Now what."

"Unless I'm crazy, this looks like…. Braille."

"Braille? Braille is raised dots."

"I'm telling you this is Braille. There's about four or five characters."

"Braille? Listen, draw the dots on a piece of paper and let me see for myself."

After a few minutes...

"Here... look for yourself."

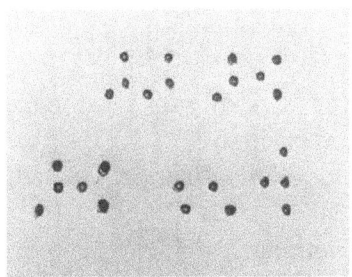

"Well, this would certainly qualify as an unusual birthmark... and it looks like I won the dominos game."

"Hey, birthmarks are brown, these are dark blue... like they were tattooed on your head or something."

"Tattooed, I never had a tattoo, I can't stand tattoos... I can't stand any invasion of the body for crying out loud."

"Well sailor... you must've been out cold drunk when this was done." Kate stated, thinking she was glad she never had her ears pierced.

"This can't be."

"How do you know this is Braille. Couldn't these be connect the dots, some perverse joke?"

"I remember from school, way back. I don't know what it means, but his is Braille."

"Pull out the laptop... let's log onto the Web... there must be a website with a Braille dictionary... just to prove you're wrong."

"Try **www.braille.com** or .org… or Google it."

"OK, OK, just a minute its loading."

"Here we go, a complete Braille alphabet…let's try to match this up."

"None of these seem to match."

"I'd swear these look like Braille characters."

"Well, here's the list… I went through Missouri once, so show me."

"It's gotta be. Here let me look at your head again."

"Would you like a crystal ball, too?"

"I've got news for you, the back of your head is starting to look like one, even without the scissors."

"OK, enough with the bald jokes. What do you see?"

"This is exactly what I see."

"Uh, I just thought of something."

"What?"

"I don't know if I want to tell you."

"What?"

"I don't want this thing going to your head, excuse the expression."

"What Edison?"

"Did you consider you might be reading my head upside down, I mean, like, this could've been put there by a Japanese Kanji Samuri or something."

"Geez, why didn't I think of that… turn around smarty pants!"

"Yes, ma'am."

"OK, now, let's try it this way. Turn your head the other way… like left side down…Here, now does this match up?"

"Oh god… I can't believe this. Let's see… now it matches the alphabet…looks like…

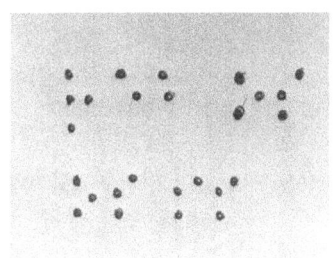

REE OS

OS SS

"How about the ROOT NAILS, are they the same letters?

"Well, actually, they do, but there are two O's, now what? Are the O's two's or three's or both, based on their sequence.

Let's see, the R=1, the E=5, another E=5, then either a two or a three, then S=0

The next line is... O= either a 2 or a 3 again, then an S=0, then two more S's, or two more O's."

155 (2or3) 0 AND 2(2or3) 00

"Sounds like it could it be the combination to a safe?"

"Could be... even with the alternative numbers, we could try the half dozen or so permutations, now just tell me which safe? Not to mention we're talking decades ago.

"Did your mother ever have a safe?"

"Nah, I can't ever remembering anyone I've known who had a real safe unless you count piggy banks? Maybe it's the combination to a chastity belt or something?"

"Real funny, Edison... and since when do you ever have to undo a chastity belt to bed a babe?"

"Well, I'm just providing options."

"How about a street address, or a telephone number. Remember, back then, the numbers didn't have area codes and oftentimes only included the last numbers?"

"Don't know... license plate?... It could be anything."

"You know what this means, don't you?"

"Not really, but I'm getting the strong impression you'll be telling me."

"Your father... Eddie 'Finger's Clark... tattooed these Braille letters on your head when you were born."

"Why?"

"That's the $64,000 question."

"Could be more like the $ 18,000,000 question."

"That's a lot of dominos we're talking about, here."

"This is getting to be a bit much. But I'm intrigued!"

"Maybe we should sleep on this and something will surface after a good night's sleep."

"Works for me, I'm bushed. I'll get the lights... see you in the morning..." and after a pause to think about it..."is that anything I need to get prepared for?" Edison joked?

No response.

"Oooh, Silence of the... good thing there's no Favre beans or Chianti around."

"That's sick, go to sleep."

"Good night Clarissa." Edison spoke, sounding like Vincent Price and not Dr. Lechter.

Kate thought, "This is good."

*   *   *

Meanwhile, in the room next door....

"Hmm… Braille? 152-20 or 30 and 22 or 23 00? You gotta love electronics." Said Tom as he pulled the suction cup off the transducer microphone off the wall abutting the adjoining room. Same thing was engraved on the inside of his mother's necklace, REE OS OS SS.

As he looked up skywards… "Pop, now you know why you couldn't get a break on this case… tattooed Braille on the kid's head… go figure!"

*   *   *

Meanwhile, in the room next to Tom…

Heavy snoring… real heavy snoring. It was a long car ride.

CHAPTER 34

Running Numbers

"So where are we going from here, asked Kate as she climbed into the rental car.

"First, I think we need to get some breakfast, second, to the hall of records in downtown Pittsburgh. I want to see if there might be a marriage or birth certificate or any other vital statistics on these characters. While I'm looking into birth and marriage/divorce records, would you check out the registry of deeds on the next floor to see if there was any unusual activity between 1932 and 1950 for any of these names." Edison asked while handing her a list of names.

"Sure... anything else we need to check out, while I'm there?"

"No, that oughta do it. Just be sure to check both the grantor and grantee indexes... OK... they should be computerized."

"Sure...listen, Edison... would you mind if we go for pizza today?" Kate interjected.

"Ah... you know... I'd prefer something... just a bit lighter for breakfast." Edison suggested facetiously, hoping for a comeback.

"And why not... breakfast IS the most important meal of the day... and pizza is THE complete food... contains all of the food groups... you know that pyramid thing... you've got your grains in the crust... the dairy and protein in the cheese... I heard that from someone."

"And your mother always told you to eat your vegetables because they're healthy for you… but not at 8 AM in the morning!"

"Hey, there are a lot of people around the world who do eat their veggies for breakfast and really enjoy them, thank you very much."

"Well, now that you mention it, I've had many a breakfast in school… cold pizza… not quite eggs Benedict, but fond memories in any case. However, enough already… but I am curious… what made you want pizza this morning."

"It's really weird, but have you ever related certain foods with certain life events?"

"You mean like birthday cake and ice cream on your birthday?" He asked sarcastically.

"I'm serious, Edison."

"Sure, I know exactly what you mean. There was this time, when…"

"Excuse me, this is my story…"

"Whoa… by all means…" Edison gestured with a flare of his right hand.

"Well, anyway… every time my family would go on a trip, my father would always want to check out the local pizza, no matter where we went… Boston, New York, the Jersey shore, Chicago… even New Haven… you name it, but the first thing was to find the best pizza place in town. Pepperoni pizza… always a pepperoni pizza. He always said you could tell a lot about a city by how they bake their pepperoni pizza… in a Blodgett or Baker's Pride gas oven, in a brick oven, using a wood fire or even a coal oven, but never on a conveyor belt… and how they cook the pepperoni.

In some cities they undercook it, others they overcook it, still others, they put in under the cheese, some thick, some thin. Now, it seems like every time I wake up in a hotel, I feel like my father is going to walk in at any moment and start talking about where we're all going for pizza later."

"Well, who knows... maybe he will..."

"My father passed on a few months ago."

"Oh..." Edison stumbled realizing his faux pas. "I'm sorry, I didn't know."

"It's OK, but that's the funny thing. It's like he's still here. I'm experiencing deja vu and feeling the same things as though he were still here and alive. It's really kind of reassuring... kind of... well... homey... knowing that your father is always still with you... that he left you part of himself... that part of him... lives on... in me... his life... his..." Kate cut herself when she realized her own faux pas. "Oh, I'm sorry Edison... I know how upset you get not knowing anything about your father and all."

"So what did your father do with the police?"

"He was a cop in Springfield... actually he was a detective... for like 40 years."

"And your brother became a cop, too?"]

"I guess it's that acorn thing not falling far from the tree."

"DNA... it's all in the DNA, I'm tellin ya."

"I'm starting to believe it."

"Sure."

"Sure, what?"

"Pizza Will be fine... for lunch." Edison added. I'll let you choose the place. I sure wouldn't want be accused of picking a pizza place that didn't turn out to be the true reflection of the social fabric of Pittsburgh... Pennsylvania.

"I'll bet someone down at the city records will know where to go." Kate nodded with certainty.

* * *

"May I take your order?" came the request from the bright red speaker with the movie marquee style menu.

"Yeah, I'd like two egg McMuffins, two coffees and a small water."

"Two Egg McMuffins, two coffees and one small water. For an extra $ 1.50 you can have juice and a potato cake with your Egg McMuffins." Came the speaker voice.

"No thanks, that will be all."

"That'll be $ 5.42. Please pull up to the first window."

"Don't worry, we'll have a nice dinner." Edison assured Kate.

* * *

After waiting almost two hours outside the county hall of records... Tom decided to go for lunch. He could always go back later and follow up on what they were looking for from the hotel... besides, Tom had already checked out the list of names a couple of years ago for leads in 'The Case' and come up with nothing.

AFTER LEAVING THE COUNTY RECORDS...

"Well, that was exciting..." Kate offered.

"Do you think Sherlock Homes was always doing exciting stuff? Detective work is 99% sweat and 1% cool stuff, or was that 1% inspiration... no, that was my Menlo Park namesake. At least we know that my parents weren't married in Pittsburgh, and that my father was born in Pittsburgh and that Weiss guy was neither born in Pittsburgh nor died in Pittsburgh and that there's no record of Harry Elam in Pittsburgh."

"And all in two hours or so... if I didn't appreciate the scientific method..."

"Seriously, every little bit we add or eliminate... well... it gets us a bit closer.

"So now I'm really hungry. Did you come up with anything for the pizza thing?"

"I sure did. Her name was Barb... she was a clerk in the registry of deeds. She told me the quintessential Pittsburgh pizza was Mineo's.

"Now that sounds promising, a lot better than a Pizza Palace." Edison offered with optimism.

"Oh, I forgot to tell you I have good news and bad news."

"OK, so do I have to pick which I want first?"

"Sorry, too late. That was the good news." Kate countered.

"And I suppose there's some bad news here, too?"

"It's on Murray Avenue."

"Wonderful, and I suppose it's right next door to Goldberg's Authentic Mexican Cantina?"

"Oh, it gets worse... Murray Ave is in a section of town... called... now get this, Squirrel Hill... I'm not making this up."

"Yes, I'll have a large pepperoni pizza and squirrel on half..." he pretended.

"Well, if you're game.... I am."

"Yuck, yuck. Hilarious. Well, how do we get there?"

"Looks like you turn off of 5th Avenue, turn left onto Forbes and keep going until you see Murray Avenue on the right. Not the fastest route, but at least we'll see some of the city instead of the highway."

"I should be able to handle that."

"Gee, can't wait…"

"Oh, come on now, if Barb the city clerk recommended it, it's got to be OK, right?"

"Sure… just like… that restaurant yesterday… Pittsburgh pizza is gonna be topped with French fries and cole slaw… and don't forget the squirrel."

"We'll check it out, OK?… besides, I'm sure they'll take the fur off, I mean they pluck the feathers off the chickens, don't they?… "

"Why do I feel like we're the one's about to get plucked shortly?"

*   *   *

"So how far away are we from Murray Avenue… I'm starved for some of that squirrel pizza anyway!"

"Follow this road around a big bend and keep going."

As Edison drove around a big bend there was a telephone pole with at least six different direction road signs… **Green Belt, Yellow Belt, Route 8, Route 22, I-376 and Pennsylvania Turnpike**.

About 10 yards after the sign pole Edison slammed on the brakes. There was a huuuge screech. The car began to tailspin... Edison dutifully and firmly turned the wheel into the skid, more screeching rubber, smoke... the car finally came to a jolting stop about six inches from a telephone pole off to the right of the street. Kate had her arms fully extended and locked up against the dashboard and her feet pumping the air on the floor as though she had a brake pedal in front of her.

"Jesus Ed, what the hell are you doing... trying to kill us... are you nuts or something?" Kate screamed... shaking like she's had just been pushed into a stone cold shower... while covering her mouth, almost bringing up her gourmet breakfast.

Edison just stared at Kate... slowly put his arm on the back of the seat, looked back through the rear window, waited for about four cars to pass, slammed the car into reverse and laid on the accelerator and burned rubber going backwards, until he could see the sign pole again.

"I'm getting out." Kate protested

"No... WAIT... LOOK!" he exclaimed, pointing to the sign pole.

"What the hell am I looking for?"

"LOOK!... Route 8 and Route 22... Pennsylvania Turnpike, I-376, Yellow... Green Belt...! So what?"

"R O U T E 8.... And R O U T E 22." He spelled out emphatically.

"Oh my god... it wasn't ROOT NAILS, it was ROUTE NAILS!!!!!!"

"You've just won a million dollahs!" exclaimed Edison in his best Regis Philbin impression.

Kate immediately loosened up and couldn't resist falling over and giving Edison a hug and hard kiss on his right cheek.

"Let's go get the squirrel pizza and figure this out." Edison beamed. You may always feel like pizza when you travel, I'm hooked on pizza whenever I have an epiphany event to celebrate.

"I'm with ya."

Mineo's was a low key place, just a few tables, a huge pizza prep table and an aroma of baking pizzas that would even make any youngster start drooling uncontrollably. They both chuckled at each other when they noticed the conspicuous absence of squirrel on the toppings menu over the prep area.

"What can I get youns?" asked the counter guy who certainly looked as though he could've been a Mineo.

"Shall we go for the pepperoni?" Asked Kate.

"That feathered cheese looks wonderful... I'd be happy with a plain cheese."

"How about half cheese half pepperoni?"

"Fine."

As they turned around to pick a table and get a couple sodas (oops... pop in Pittsburgh) Kate shrieked..."THOMAS DUGAN... WHAT IN THE HELL ARE YOU DOING HERE?"

Tom's shoulders fell and his head hung as though he had just been caught with his hand in the cookie jar... and he did.

"Aaaaah..." he stammered.

"Don't tell me this is some kind of macho big brother thing, please... you didn't make some kind of deal with Daddy to do this, like that time he tailed me on that overnight trip to New York I took with Rudy... ah geez... you swine, why can't you trust me... Daddy never followed you around, did he... NO he didn't. Don't you have anything better to do with your time... besides, weren't you supposed to be investigating that old guy back in Springfield for Edison? Why aren't you answering me?"

Tom thought to himself..."Sis, that's exactly what I am doing.", knowing that Hack was parked down the street several stores down... hard to miss that big Caddy... but he couldn't bring himself to tell her the truth, so he applied basic truth avoidance maneuvers, since Kate was the one who set the foundation... "Well, I admit it is a dual standard..."

"Well, my butt... I want you out of here on the next stagecoach, do you understand, mister?"

"Ah, can I at least finish my pizza?"

As sometimes is the case, extreme anger can turn instantly on a dime to laughter in the right circumstances.

"You too, eh... let me guess... pepperoni pizza?"

"Gee, I thought you'd never ask?" Tom admitted. "And you?"

"Only half pepperoni... I got the other half cheese." Edison chimed in.

"Oh, I see, telling the outsiders all the family secrets, huh?

"You know if I weren't so damn mad at you, I'd really be laughing right now... but seeing you here, of all places, away from home, pizza joint...it's just... so... Daddy. And just how did you come to pick this place?" Kate asked.

"Pittsburgh.com... listed it as one of the top pizzas in town."

"And just how long have you been here?"

"Got here yesterday."

"And just where are you…?"

"So… how about those Pirates… or is it the Steelers…?" Tom interrupted so as not to get into a dicey area of conversation.

"I don't want to get in the middle of a family thing here, but I did want to thank you for finding Evan." Edison offered.

"Don't mention it... just doing my job."

After woofing down his remaining piece and gulping the last of his drink, Tom admitted, "I'm really sorry, Sis… I didn't realize until this very moment just how stupid an idea this was… it's this detective stuff… the need to know… you're right… I'm dead wrong… it's your life and I have no right whatsoever… I'll be heading out of here, like immediately."

Tom paused before leaving waiting for a response from Kate, and he got the one he hoped for… a brotherly hug and a tug on his cheek.

"Hrumph." She mumbled.

Tom left and quickly got into his dark blue rental car.

Edison saw the car and realized that Tom had been following them from the time they got to Pittsburgh. He didn't notice the Caddy following behind. "This is more than just an overly protective brother." Edison thought. "He's here for the coins, too… hmmmm… If the detective is looking for the coins too… and was too embarrassed to say anything about it… something's squirrelly around here and it's not the pizza. And if Tom is skulking around, that Hacksaw guy can't be far away either… and all those computer tracing tags and cookies Will was telling me about… it was Kate's brother…. Oh shit!"

"How did Tom know we were in Pittsburgh, did you tell him?" Edison inquired carefully.

"I'm sorry Edison, I did tell my mom and I'm sure she told Tom to check up on me."

That made Edison feel a little better, but not much. It all started making sense to him, all the loose ends were coming together.

Kate and Edison settled into a table next to the window. Kate pulled out the paper with the Braille on it.

"Do you believe the nerve of that guy... so if we use ROUTE NAILS, what do we have?" She forced herself to ask in order to avoid any more discussion about her overly protective brother. "Looks like 155 20... and 20 00... what do you make of that?"

"I've never heard of a safe with a number over 99."

"155 20... 20 00?... can't be the year 2000, too far away to be tattooed on your head in the 60's."

Edison kept looking at the map of Italy over the table, anticipating the arrival of the pizza.

"Ed, are you here or in Italy?"

"I'm here... just trying to process."

155 20... 20 00... 155 20... 20 00... 155 20... 20 00.

Edison and Kate were staring at each other, half glazed over trying to make sense of the numbers.

"Why would my father tattoo 155 20 and 20 00 on my head?... and in code...?"

"It's got to be the clue to where the gold coins are... gotta be."

"I can't disagree, but these numbers aren't going to help unless we figure out what they mean or where they come from."

Finally, the pizza came. After one bite... all they could do was eat... pulling the cheese in strings from the pizza and trying not to get it all over themselves. This pizza was great! Edison was right. There was something different about the cheese... wow!" For a moment, they actually forgot about the numbers. After the entire pizza was devoured, reality returned.

"I'm going nuts, here, what do we do?"

"It's got to be logical... come on... let's not give up...it looks like a two sets of two different numbers, right?"

"Yeah."

"So, what could 155 20 mean?"

"155 paces... marks the spot... 155 feet... 155 yards... 155 miles... 155 what?... what goes together in two sets of numbers?"

"Blank and blank..."

"Revolutions per minute... miles per hour... hours and minutes... minutes and seconds... Laurel and Hardy, for crying out loud."

"What fits for 155?... Angles are 90 degrees, a line is 180 degrees, a circle is 360 degrees."

"Hey, aren't airport runways marked by degrees.?"

"Yeah, but they drop off the zero's... and each end of the runway is a difference of 18, or 180 degrees... half a circle for each direction of the runway."

"Wait.... half a circle, a compass, all these numbers fit within a compass... that would be some kind of direction, wouldn't it?"

"Sounds good, let's go with that."

"A compass direction... wait... don't those GPS handheld gadgets read out in compass directions... yeah, in latitude and longitude... BINGO... 155 could be a longitude or a latitude in degrees... and the 20 could be the minutes... they go in increments of 60, 60 minutes per degree."

"Fits... could be."

"We need a map, quick."

They looked out of the window... and across the street was a small store called, 'GAMES UNLIMITED'.

"They have to have some kind of map over there, let's go."

*   *   *

Bob the 'Hat Guy' was perched on a stool behind the counter. The store was loaded to the rafters with just about every game ever invented.

"Hey, how are you doing?" Bob asked. It was more than just the typical sales lead in. In fact, Edison felt recognized, but they had never met before.

"Hi... a... listen... any chance you'd have a map here, showing the latitudes and longitudes.?"

"You going orienteering?"

"Ah, no not really." Edison replied

"Well, I've got all kinds of maps, with games, globes, you name it."

"You've got a globe?"

"Sure, right over there."

"Great... mind if we check it out."

"Go right ahead. If you need some help, just yell."

Edison and Kate huddled together... scouring over the globe.

"Let's see… 155 has to be longitude, broken down in 180 East and West degrees… and the 20 must be latitude, I know we live around 42 degrees North…."

"155 is in the Pacific West or East… great… I think we hit a dead end."

"Hold on, where is it exactly?"

"There's 150 and there's 165 East… Right in the middle of the ocean. Let's see, 155 West…

"What's the latitude… 20 degrees and 00 minutes?"

"Yeah, the equator is 0, the tropic of Cancer is about 25, so a little bit south… oh my god…"

"Aloooha!"

"Hawaii…. Pineapple… Weiss's girlfriend. Where exactly in Hawaii are we?"

"The Big Island… looks like the closest town is….. Laupahoehoe."

"Did I just hear you say…Hoity… Hoity…something… Miss Louise?"

It was an involuntary hug… it couldn't be stopped… it was merely the expression and the outlet and release from the stress…

Bob the Hat Guy looked over shaking his head and laughed… "I've never seen a globe cause such euphoria before… this doesn't have anything to do with that orb thing from Woody Allen's Sleeper movie, does it?"

"No, No, were just happy about solving a mystery."

"Well if a globe can do that and solve a mystery, I've got some real mystery games… but I won't assume any liability for what they might cause you guys to do!"

Bob obviously noticed it… and for the first time… Edison noticed it, too. Something was different, very different between the two of them.

They thanked Bob the Hat Guy profusely, and left somehow realizing that Bob was some sort of catalyst or lightning rod. They would never forget him.... Bob the Hat guy... even though they never knew his last name.

* * *

They got back into the car... stared at one another...and they both said the word simultaneously...

"Hawaii!"

"Let's get back to the motel... we can get tickets online."

"What in the world are we going to do once we get there?"

"What in the world did we plan on doing here in Pittsburgh?"

"Point well taken."

"Ooooh, how do you feel about pineapple on your pizza? The Hawaiian pizza is really good... one of the few fond memories when I was in Hawaii before.

"As long as it has pepperoni... who cares?

"Do you think Tom will follow us?"

"No way... he's learned his lesson."

"Waikiki... Don Ho... Steve McGarrett... Magnum PI...here we come."

"Should we really get tickets... today?"

"Book'em Danno."

* * *

Edison logged on the internet while Kate began packing her things up in the bathroom. Tom slipped in the adjoining room and activated his spy software, which was only able to mirror Edison's screen when he was logged on via a dial-up connection. Tom knew there was some connection with 'The Case' in Hawaii, but was unclear of its importance until Edison went on Priceline.com to request two airline tickets to Honolulu. While he was waiting for the results, Edison typed in his search engine… "Laupahoehoe, HI", the results were mirrored on Tom's computer.

When Edison saw that Laupahoehoe was located on the Big Island, Edison realized he made a mistake and hoped his bid for airline tickets to Honolulu (on the island of Oahu) would be rejected, because it looked like he should have booked into either Kona or Hilo on the Big Island. Within five minutes, Edison got the bad news… his bid was accepted and they were locked into going to Honolulu and would have to catch an inter-island flight to the Big Island.

Tom knew that some catastrophe was involved with the missing coins. Tom's father Ernie had documented some telegrams that took place in 1946 that referred to the loss of the Hawaiian woman due to some natural catastrophe like a typhoon or tsunami. The telegrams were coded to be vague and he never knew the significance of the catastrophe, but Tom was able to put the pieces together when he read about the tsunami catastrophe that took place in Laupahoehoe in April, 1946 on the Web.

Tom immediately booked a flight to Hilo, HI through Chicago. Finally, he thought he caught a real break. Getting into Hilo would give him at least a half day lead. He thought to himself if he could only find some clue in Laupahoehoe, he might be able to get the jump on the coins as he already figured out the numbers were indeed longitude and latitude coordinates as soon as he heard the braille clues and tied that to the mother's locket. He then remembered that the evidence his father gathered referred to Laupahoehoe Point and it hit him a few minutes later that the screen from Edison's last search listed Laupahoehoe Point. He immediately went back and got the link referring to the devastating tsunami on April 1, 1946.

Tom deduced that the coins were washed somehow into the ocean from their hiding place on shore and that it was unlikely anyone was aware of the existence of the coins since their existence was certainly not advertised and that it was likely that the person who hid the coins was one of the victims and that the Web Site indicated there was no swimming at the park. When Tom scrolled down to view the enlarged view of the Laupahoehoe Point memorial listing all the names of the victims, he knew this was it. One of the names on the memorial stone matched with a name in Ernie Dugan's records.

All he needed was some snorkel gear and a waterproof metal detector.

*   *   *

Tom finally checked for other links to web sites on the Big Island. He knew he would have to hire a helicopter for a bird's eye view to survey the beach and ocean area off Laupahoehoe Point and to rent some snorkeling gear. Tom was upset that he never took SCUBA lessons. He knew that the snorkeling might not be adequate if the depth of the ocean floor dropped off from the shore much and he certainly didn't want to have to hire a SCUBA diver to help out… the fewer people involved the better… and he only had a half day time advantage, maybe a day if he was lucky. Tom was annoyed that the names provided on the Big Island Links site did not actually link directly to the web sites for the helicopter and SCUBA businesses. He had to access the yellow pages site to get telephone numbers.

"Things are definitely falling into place… finally!" Tom thought to himself. "If only Pop could be here to see me now." Tom suddenly stopped and could do nothing but sit on the edge of the bed and re-live the cacophony of emotions from his father's funeral… the sadness… the anger from the comments of the other detectives… the determination… the revenge… the determination… the loss… solve 'The Case'.

"Pop…We're gettin close… real close… We're gonna do   this,   promise."

*   *   *

Hacksaw followed Tom to the airport and was surprised when his bags were being checked to Hilo, HI. Tom made sure Hack would find out he was going to Hawaii. He felt if Hack would also go to Hilo, he might be able to put the final pieces of the original robbery into place given that Hack was probably the only surviving person involved with it and also that he might need Hack to de-rail Edison, so he could get to the coins, first. Mussner was from Hilo and he now knew that's where the coins must have gone.

One huge, gigantic problem… there's no highway to Hilo… Hack almost bust a gut when he realized he would have to actually get on an airplane… he almost had a nervous breakdown when he realized he would have to be on an airplane… 9 hours. This was going to take copious amounts of alcohol before, during, and after such an excursion, but his son Roger, was worth it.

CHAPTER 35

Rolling a Pair a Dice

Tom disembarked from the airplane and was surprised there was no jetway or other mechanical equipment found at most every other modern airport in the world. Tom almost expected to see Humphrey Bogart or some other icon from the old black and white days pop out from behind one of the thatched hutted gazebos dotting the perimeter of the airport. It was totally in the open, airy and Tom thought, "Gee, what a difference from New England, even in the summer. Ah, paradise. This is what they must be talking about. He was carrying his laptop computer and a small carry on suitcase with wheels with his limited clothing, more suitable for New England than paradise.

Tom retrieved his bag and quickly half ran up to the rental car hut to pick up the car he arranged for over the internet.

"Aloha, Welcome to de Big Island." Mona proudly announced. "Are you coming from the mainland?" she inquired, seeing Tom dressed in tan khaki pants and a permanent pressed short sleeved buttoned down blue oxford cloth shirt which had been through several too many washings.

"Yes, my name is Dugan, that's D U G A N", he spelled out for her a bit abruptly.

Mona sensed that Tom needed to acclimate to an island pace and to unwind a bit and began by asking, "Is this your first time to Hawai'i?" as she began to type his name into the computer. "An may I please see your driver's license?"

"Yes, I requested a mid size car." Tom responded in a businesslike fashion, not wanting the tourist treatment.

"Ya ya." Mona commented as she was alternating between her computer and Tom. "We have a red Mustang convertible available… and it would only cost you $8 per day extra and you would be able to enjoy our fantastic sun while you are here. Are you here for business… or vacation?" Mona asked with just a hint more than professional courtesy,

Tom, sensing he was getting the tourist treatment and being anxious to get things moving, pulled out his badge and stated,

"I'm here on official business, please, if we could move things along."

Mona gazed at the badge, seeing it was from Massachusetts commented, "Oooh, my brudda is a cop in Hilo, none of that Hawaii 5-0 stuff though." "Anything he might be able to do for you?"

"No thanks."

"Well, then, here is his card, just in case, and do you have a place to stay, yet?"

"Actually, no, I was surprised there seemed to be only a few motels in the Hilo area."

"Well, here is another card for the Best Hawaiian Inn. My sister Robin works the front desk. Tell her you're a cop and that I sent you and she'll give you the kama'ina rates."

Tom thought, "Hmmmm. Kama'ina rates must be the tourist rip off rates. Its seems like everybody is related to everyone else around here."

Tom then said, "Thanks, I'll check it out." "Can I just have a basic mid size car and I'll be on my way."

Mona, sensing she wasn't getting anywhere here, either with Tom or the upgrade, she asked "Do you want the pre-paid fuel option where you can bring the car back empty, or would you prefer to pay for fuel as you go and return the car full?"

Tom, realizing that most people would opt for the more costly convenience of bringing the car with whatever fuel was left, but having already paid for a full tank answered, "I'll pay for my own gas, thanks."

Mona asked pointing to various lines on the form, "Would you please sign here and here, and initial here, here and here." "You have the silver Taurus in space 18." We are temporarily out of mid size cars, so I upgraded you to a full size car at no charge."

"Thanks." Tom responded, taking the keys and began looking to the left down the parking lot for #18.

"Aloha and enjoy your stay in Hawai'i.! Mona cheerfully threw out for one last possible reaction. There was none.

CHAPTER 36

A Family Affair

Tom was driving with the street map of Hilo pressed against the steering wheel, when he saw a street sign, "Kamehameha Ave."

Tom glanced at the card Mona had given him.

Best Hawaiian Inn
18 Kamehameha Ave.
Hilo, HI
Robin Jackson, Day Manager
808-555-1016

"What the hell.." He thought…"Maybe I'll need some help from the local department… might be worth it even if I get ripped off a little on the hotel price…"

*   *   *

"Aloha… may I help you?" Asked the receptionist at the Best Hawaiian Inn.
"Yeah… I'll need a room for a few days… how much are they?"
"Are you silver Taurus Tom?" She asked already knowing that he was… looking out the window to the parking lot at the silver Taurus.

"Jeez… I feel like I'm under a microscope here… tight community, eh…" Tom thought to himself. "…and you must be….Robin?" he asked.

Tom noticed that Robin was a rather tallish athletic looking thirty something with green eyes a very engaging smile and straight shoulder length dark hair dressed in a aloha shirt over a mid calf blue skirt, with a flower in the right side of her head.

"Of course… really… my sister Mona works the car rental desk at the airport and clued me in…. she said you were a cop….and cute… and said to make sure I gave you the kama'ina rates."

All Tom initially heard was "cute", but momentarily heard that other word… kama'ina and asked…"Just what is a kama'ina rate, anyway, double the usual price, for an unsuspecting   tourist?"

"No…No.. kama'ina rates are the ones we give to local residents, so they can afford to come to a motel without going broke competing with the tourist bucks… really… it'll be 33% less than the lowest advertised price on the internet."

"In that case, sounds like a deal."

"Are you traveling alone…" she paused waiting for the anticipated desired response.

"Yes, just one."

"And would you like a non-smoking or smoking room?"

"Non-smoking."

"Good…" Robin nodded while she entered some data in the computer. "And how will you be paying…"

"Here's my credit card…but I'm guessing you already have my number… from Mona?" Tom offered, kidding.

"Well… I do have to run it through the machine… " she responded playfully.

"You'll be in room 323, overlooking the ocean, will you need only one card?

"Yeah... one will do.."

"We have a pool in the back and a 24 hour restaurant over to the left, if you're hungry later.... say...after 5...?"

Tom was just too tired and oblivious to the come on...

"Actually, I'm going to need some snorkeling gear and maybe a boat or even a helicopter... and a waterproof metal detector.... I don't suppose you would happen to know..."

"You're not going to believe this... but .... my father owns Captain Jacks over toward the park... he can probably help you out with all that stuff...and I can see if he'll give you kama'ina rates... too..."

Tom just shook his head, thinking..."I give up... you just can't beat this place..." then said...

"Actually I do believe it, in fact I'd be surprised if you didn't have a father in the business... and your mother?"

"Oh, she sells real estate.... Staying awhile?" She asked hopefully.

"Finally, someone in the family who won't be selling me something." Tom thought. "Just where does Captain Jack hang out?" He asked.

"Do you know your way around here?"

"Not really, but I'm good with a map."

"Why don't you go to your room and unwind, I'll be off at five... and if you'd like, I'll take you over there."

Exhausted from the long flight and fighting the 'system' around here, he relented. "OK... why not... should I stop by around 5?"

"I'll be ready at 5:01"

"See you then." Tom walked off toward the elevator down the hall.

CHAPTER 37

The Pilot's Son

"Your car or mine?" Robin asked.

"Well, I've got unlimited mileage, might as well use mine, unless you think Mona would mind. Will she be there?"

"No, she's working all evening at the airport."

"That's not what I was going for." Tom thought...expecting to see the whole family there. "Is there anyone else in the family I should know about?

"Just my brother Harley... but he won't be there... he and my father don't get along too well.... Some kind of macho male competitive thing."

Tom finally letting his interest out a bit asked, "So... is this a family motel or is it just a job?"

"Oh, I'm just working there until I get my degree... I'm on the 15 year plan at the University of Hawaii – Hilo.'

"What are you studying?"

"A kind of Bio-Horticulture thing... I'm really into orchids and want to create new variations and growing environments. They are a big business here on the Big Island."

"How did you get into that?"

"Well, I was never asked to my own prom, and I felt I missed something by not getting flowers, so..."

"I can't believe no one asked you to the prom, you're kidding me aren't you?"

"No really... back then I was kind of a tom boy...actually I still am... I just can't get into lipstick and makeup and all that crap. I was raised with engine oil, not perfume... my Dad's into motorcycles, helicopters and that stuff."

"Jeez, is that where Harley came from."

"Ooh... and he's a good detective, too!" she cooed while she gently slapped Tom on the leg. "Yeah... I swear he was conceived in Milwaukee."

"So you're not originally from around here?"

"Ya ya, my parents moved here after Viet Nam... my dad was stationed here with the Air Force over at Hickam Air Force Base on Oahu and decided to stay. He didn't like the crowds over there so he moved to Hilo and opened his helicopter business for the tourists. There's a lot of money to be made flying the haoles around the volcanoes over at the Kilauea caldera over at Mauna Loa... where the eruptions are."

"So, your Dad's a pilot?"

"Yeah, are you going to need a ride?"

"Maybe."

"Touring the Island?"

"No, I may need a helicopter for a little investigative work I need to do while I'm here."

"In that case, you might want to see my brother... Harley."

"I doubt I'll be needing a motorcycle."

"No... well, he does have one for rent, but no... he's a pilot too... pretty good one. He's a little cocky, just the type to do a little detective work, but don't say anything to my dad... they've got this thing going on... Harley went and opened his own helicopter touring business part time... and my dad is furious" as she pointed to the sign on the storefront as they pulled in.

"CAPTAIN JACK'S ~~AND SON~~"

"Oh…" Tom commented, seeing the light.

CHAPTER 38

A Heart of Gold

"Hi Pop..." Announced Robin as she walked into the shop.

Fred Jackson was a tall outdoorsy type, in good shape, with long salt and pepper hair tied back in a ponytail, wearing a leather vest, blue jeans and wire rimmed reading glasses. He looked up over the half glasses from a stack of invoices he was checking.

"Hi Hon...what...or ...should I say who brings you in?" He winked as they gave each other a brief hug over the counter.

"This is Tom Dugan... " Robin offered as they shook hands.

"Nice to meet you Mr. Jackson."

"Call me Fred...Are you two an item?"

"C'mon Pop... He just came in from the Mainland and is staying at the hotel...he's a cop." Robin jumped in.

"Now what did I do?" Fred asked half joking, half defensively.

"He needs some snorkeling gear, a metal detector... and maybe a boat." Robin chimed in.

"You'll have to excuse her…" Fred stopped her.. "She's like her mother… likes to take charge, but has a heart of gold." he added as he sensed there might be a little more than met the eye from her eye contact with Tom.

Tom thought…"Curious choice of words…gold…but.." then added…"Yeah, I'm doing a little research on a case from back home… may need to get into the water a bit."

"Where do you need to put in?"

"Some place up the road a bit…Laa..u..pa … hoe..hoe.park?"

"Laupahoehoe?

"Yeah, that sounds like it could be it."

"You mean where the tsunami hit back in '46?

"Yeah, that's the place."

"It's pretty rocky out there… lots of lava chunks… this has nothing to do with the tsunami… does it, I mean they pretty much cleaned up afterwards and all, not much in the way of snorkeling or scuba… no wrecks or anything…

"I just need to tie up a few loose ends….Actually, it might be better to take a pass over the area by air, just to get my bearings?"

"No problem, it's a short run over there, let's see. I've got a couple bookings toward the weekend, but I could pencil you in tomorrow morning if you want."

"That would be great."

"Well, I can set you up with anything else you need… looks like you've got a rental… all this diving stuff should fit in there without any problem, except for the boat… you need a skipper?"

"I'll take it out for him…" Robin volunteered…"And I work cheap… dinner…lunch…. movie…?" she provided options.

Tom just realized he was the bait and that he was just hooked... and... he didn't really mind. He was never aggressive when it came to affairs of the heart and Robin's forward behavior was actually welcomed... not to mention she was definitely his type, but he wasn't going to allow anything to get in his way...he's much too close... maybe she could be of some help, so why not...

"OK... This isn't going to be one of those three-hour tours that go terribly awry and we end up on some deserted island?" Tom asked as they were leaving the store, seeing if she would pick up on the Gilligan's Island joke.

"Soo... Gilligan, would that be soooo bad?"

"She's good." Thought Tom.

"Hey, it's getting late, want to grab some dinner... I know a nice place... fresh fish..."

"Don't tell me... it's your uncle's place."

"Nah...what do you think... we're all related to each other.... It's my old roommates place." Freshest Mahi Mahi on the Island."

CHAPTER 39

Like Father Like Son

As they looked over the menu, Robin suggested, "OK, I'll make a deal with you…you try the *Big Island Mahi Mahi* and I'll get the *baked stuffed shrimp*… and if you don't like what you get, I'll switch with you… otherwise, we can share, deal?"

"OK…OK… I give up… deal."

"So, are you going to tell me exactly why you've come to Hawai'i?"

Tom paused momentarily, then decided to tell her just enough to satisfy her natural curiosity…

"Well, it's a long story, but in a nutshell, my father was a cop, too…"

"Like father , like son…. Know the story…"

"Anyway, he had this case… all the way back in the '30s which he was never able to solve and I kind of picked up the pieces when he retired. "

"So, this is kind of like Lt. Gerard dogging Richard Kimble?"

Tom realized she was definitely a child of the television era…"Well, it's more of a robbery case than murder, although a couple people have met an early demise in this thing."

"So, what was stolen?"

"Some merchandise stored in a crate."

"They must be valuable."

"Maybe, maybe not... but it's more about putting a period at the end of this case... made a promise to my dad."

"Is your father with you?"

"He passed on a few months ago."

"Sorry."

"Feel like I owe him."

"Did the two of you get along?"

"Oh, no problem there, although he spent a lot of time at work."

"Sounds like my dad and Harley, until recently."

"What's the deal there?"

"My dad was military, flew helicopter missions in Viet Nam... and after the war, came here to the Big Island and set up a tourist business, helicopter tours over the volcanoes and around the island, then got into rentals, well you saw it..."

"So your dad loved Harleys and ..."

"Yeah, my mom thought he was crazy for naming him after a motorcycle, but they already had me, and when a boy came along, well, since he proposed to her on one...she just gave in."

"...and well, my dad and Harley are a lot alike... Harley joined the national guard as a helicopter pilot...but my dad wanted him to go to college and get a degree, become a lawyer or a CPA...."

"He didn't want him to become a doctor?"

"Nah... that was the big joke that he wasn't pressuring him THAT much. Anyway, Harley hated school and they fought every night over homework, grades, you name it. All Harley wanted to do was to be like his dad, and fly. Every time my dad signed him up for baseball, or football, or soccer, he would quit before the season was over. Every time Harley had a science project or a term paper, he wouldn't finish it, so my dad starting calling him a 'quitter'. I know he loved him, and was just trying to motivate him, but Harley took it hard and they just fought all the time, you know, dad wanting him to act and be something and Harley wanting to do his own thing, on his own terms... well, after my dad put up that sign at the store, you know... and Son... without asking him about it, well Harley freaked out and left... he just didn't want to be in Captain Jack's shadow any longer. He became a cop in Hilo. They haven't spoken since. Ironic, though... they are almost like identical now.

"Sounds like my dad and me, except I liked school!"

"Here are your meals." the server offered.

"Tom gazed at his platter... macadamia nut encrusted pan grilled mahi mahi complemented with a pineapple and red pepper salsa. He was surprised that he actually liked it.

"Ironic... the pineapple." He thought.

"And what's this?" he asked about the light purple juice being poured into his glass.

"That's guava juice... it will settle your stomach, good before and after being out on the ocean."

CHAPTER 40

A New Set of Choppers

Harley pulled on the control stick and firmly pressed the rudder pedal and swung the copter around facing the shore, about 50 yards off the shoreline along Laupahoehoe Point park.

The sun was now off to the port side and Harley asked "So… do you know where you want to jump in?"

Edison looked at the faded photograph he got from his mother and tried turning it around and around until he was able to align the picture with the rock formations and water below. It was hard since the picture was taken slightly above ground level and here he was trying to pinpoint the location from 20 feet in the air.

"Yeah, I think we have to go over there, about another 20 yards." Edison said pointing to the southeast.

As they approached the area, Edison's heart started pounding. There it was… momentarily, a peak of lava sticking out of the surf that looked like a pineapple! As quickly as it exposed itself, it had returned below the surf, out of sight.

"Keep your eye on that spot." Edison thought to himself. The constantly changing surf mesmerized Edison such that he had great difficulty trying to maintain his focus on the spot where the lava peak was intermittently above, then below the surf.

"Is this it?" Harley barked out.

"I think so… can you lower this so I can slide out?"

"I can do whatever you want, pal." Harley responded. "It's your choice, but the closer I put this baby near the water, the bumpier it'll get... the back draft can get pretty rough and the rocks down there are sharp like razors that'll slice you up like a salami if you're not careful."

Harley pushed on the rudder, pulled on the control stick and turned the chopper around 180 degrees so that now he was facing the northwest. He was now holding the chopper and hovering, waiting for Edison to get everything together, before he began his descent close to water so that Edison could slide out as easily as possible.

While Harley was hovering, another helicopter became visible from around the rocky curved shoreline. "What the...." Harley exclaimed.

It was an Astar super 350, red and white, painted with orchids along the side. "We've got trouble." Harley announced.

"Trouble?" Edison returned in a shaky voice.

"Yeah... it's my dad... he's been bucking for a fight for awhile now... I can see... this could get ugly."

"It looks like he's got a passenger, too." remarked Edison as he was able to see Tom in the passenger seat.

Harley edged his helicopter directly facing Fred and Tom, about 50 yards from the shoreline and 20 feet above the water surface and 100 yards between them. Edison could clearly make out the three propeller blades on the Astar. Both helicopters, squared off directly in front of each other, eye to eye, mano a mano, father to son... and now, son to son and father to father... as though Ernie and Artie were there with them... but really... they were.

Edison was sitting in the passenger seat, holding his diving flippers and sitting at an angle so that the smallish air tank was not jammed into the seatback.

CHAPTER 41

Joust In Time

"I don't like the look on his face." Harley commented as they continued to hover and stare each other down. "I've seen that look before...he looks like he's got something to prove to me."

"What do you think he's going to do?" Edison asked.

"I don't know... he's a man with a hot temper ...and nerves as cold as steel... Viet Nam MASH vet... not a good combination if you're trying to avoid trouble, if you know what I mean."

"Exactly what do you mean?"

"I'm not the type to back down from a fight, even if it's my old man... "

Just before Harley was able to get the words out, Fred engaged his chopper forward directly in the path of Harley and Edison.

"He's coming directly at us!" Edison exclaimed.

"Yes he is. " Harley responded, matter of fact... as he tightened up on the control stick, his hand slightly shaking, not from fright, but firmly in control and being prepared to respond at the drop of a dime.

Edison turned white as a sheet and held his breath. It looked like Tom in the other chopper was just as white. As Fred got closer and closer ... the noise of both engines now becoming deafening...and....he closed his eyes and scrunched his face waiting to be hit.

Fred's chopper veered at the last possible moment, nearly grazing Fred, missing him by less than 6 inches. There was a brief, but severe buffeting from the wind generated by Harley's copter. A couple beads of sweat rolled down Harley's face, but he was still in control.

"What the hell have I gotten myself into, here…" Edison thought.

Fred maintained his position, still hovering, as Harley swerved around and assumed the same position he had before this chicken run.

"He thinks I'll back down, but I'm not budging." Harley stated… "Listen, it might be better if I drop you off now."

"Works for me." Edison replied, faced with the fear of jumping in the water with unknown jagged lava rocks or getting rammed by another helicopter mid-air, the water seemed the much lesser evil.

"I'm going down… get ready."

Edison arranged his gear and slid the door open, thinking as he watched the water surface get closer and closer. "This is not what I had in mind for my first Hawaiian open water dive." The chopper was bouncing around due to a strong reflective updraft and Edison was reliving every last exam question he had taken earlier for his PADI training exam.

"You better go now." Growled Harley.

Edison slid out onto the strut and immediately slipped off and into the ocean surf quite by accident. But for the slip, he would have paused several moments to get his nerve, but now, that was history.

Edison hit the surf as his tank caused a stiff jolt, but immediately he felt safe... no lava rocks. His first thought was that the water was much warmer that he had envisioned. With his nerves on high alert, he just expected the surf would be New England chilly. It felt soothing as he floated on the surface, feeling the gusty breeze being created by Harley as he slowly revved up to gain altitude. Slowly the heavy breeze dwindled as Harley gained altitude.

Edison immediately placed his respirator in his mouth, something he forgot to do in his hasty exit from the helicopter, but he just bobbed in the surf, slowly working his fins back on his feet and treading water, watching the two helicopters assume their previous positions. "I'm OK, he thought... what are those idiots going to do up there?"

He immediately and instinctively began to swim away toward the shore to get out of the way, if any of those birds came down.

On the beach, Robin was yelling at the top of her lungs, "You idiots... what the hell are you doing.... You're going to kill each other...stop it... stop it..." and fell to her knees in the sand at water's edge, unable to do anything. No one in the helicopters could hear. Kate was just arriving to the point and came up to her to provide some much needed support. She continued to sob with her hands over her face, muttering.

CHAPTER 42

Second Pass

Harley was waiting to see if Fred was going to drop off his passenger, but he wasn't budging.

The two helicopters once again aligned in front of each other... Fred edged his forward once, then twice and a third time. Harley suddenly edged forward a bit. The scene was set.

Robin just sat back on the sand.

"Look at them. They think they're medieval knights or something, in some kind of medieval jousting duel."

Indeed they were. Both knights ... one youthful, the other experienced...both fully armored... aboard their powerful steeds with horsepower to spare... spinning propeller blades, whirring in the late morning sun.

The flags were flapping in the wind... the trumpets were blaring out... the crowd noise.... Cheering.... The wind blowing.... And as if the king had just dropped the flag....

Both helicopters revved up ... and started toward each other.

It took a moment for each copter to get up to speed.... They reached speed.... Closing on each other.... Directly in line with one another...closer... closer.... closer still...neither yielding.

The whirring metal propeller blades ticked each other... a bright flash... a spark, almost like a mini lightning bolt shot out from the two helicopters...

Fortunately, both Harley and Fred both instinctively pulled the control stick toward them and simultaneously pushed the left rudder pedal and each veered off to their respective left. If either of them had not instinctively reacted the same, they certainly would have crashed... head on... and most certainly died. Anyone other than a father and son wouldn't have been so lucky.

But here they were... once again... lined up... Harley positioned... hovering... facing now to the southeast.... Fred hovering... facing now to the northwest.... Paused.... Poised....

And both knowing how each other reacted during the last pass.

"Do I react the same way... or do I anticipate Fred will react differently ..." Harley pondered.

"I need to teach this kid a lesson, he'll never forget..." Fred thought. He revved up.

Harley revved up...

Neither knight had been knocked off... so... honor demanded yet another charge.

Medieval history shows that the true challenge in a joust was to hold your line... not to hesitate.... Not to veer off.... Not to wimp out.....Both Harley and Fred realized they did wimp out at the very last split second during the last pass...that may have been prudent.... but it was not chivalrous....it was not fearless... it would not happen again.

It would be highly unlikely for both Harley and Fred to react the same way as the last pass.

The next charge would be different....one way or the other.

CHAPTER 43

Third Time's a Charm

Tom's t-shirt was drenched with sweat. As a cop, he had thought he'd seen most tense situations... but this.... pure medieval. He knew he was stuck in this situation for the duration. There was no way out... The first pass... well, he knew that there would be no problem... that was for show.... That was the dropping of the glove.... That was the challenge. The second charge, well... that was another matter.... The survival instinct took over and both Harley and Fred avoided disaster.... This third charge? "What's the worst that could happen if I jump from up here?" He thought. He wouldn't have the time to follow through on that thought.

The exhaust fumes from both engines looked like the warm exhalations from the horses on a chilly afternoon. The engines roared, the flying horses bucked, revved up and started toward each other, both holding their line. Closer... closer... and...

The propeller blades caused a screeching sound when they became entangled, causing flying sparks in all directions, like the finale at a fourth of July fireworks celebration. Both helicopters bounced off one another and got caught together in their landing struts.

As each copter spun around connected to each other, like they were doing a Virginia reel, hand in hand. The propellers finally came to a grinding squealing halt looking like a hot molten spaghetti and the entwined birds fluttered, round and round until they hit the surf with a huge thud. They both bounced off the surf one time and then came down hitting the surf a second time and began sinking in the water.

CHAPTER 44

Drink Anyone?

"How appropriate!" was the last thought Hack had as he sat in the boat watching the tangled mass of metal remaining from the propellers spinning and coming at him at about 300 rpm 10 feet directly above. In less than a second, the slicing propellers from the tail rotor slashed across his chest, killing him instantly.

As the two fuselages from the helicopters were spinning out of control just above the blue surf, Robin hysterically dove into the surf and began swimming out

Kate quickly strapped on her air tank, flippers and turned on her regulator and half ran to the edge of the surf.

"Whoa." She thought and stopped in her tracks. She paused a moment, took the regulator out of her mouth, turned around and ran back to the chairs. She immediately grabbed her cell phone and dialed "911".

"Hello!....Hello!"... she nearly screamed into the phone....

"Yes.... Yes... there's been a terrible accident...two helicopters, they're both down... crashed... in the ocean... together... hurry... please....yes.... aahh.... Lau...pahoehoe park....where the tsunami monument is... On the Big Island...oh....OK.... Yessss.....there were three people in the copters, one in a boat and one scuba diver in the ocean.... Yeah.... Where it crashed..... yeah... you better send several ambulances.... FAST!....no....I have to go in to help.....OK....I'll leave the phone on....."

"Wow...what a weird noise...." Edison thought as he furiously pumped his legs trying to get to where he saw a tornado of sand swirling as though a bomb had just exploded as the two fuselages slammed into the bottom of the ocean, about 20 feet below the surface and about 30 yards from his position. Then a mangled web of propeller blades still spinning in the water, like a dough hook on high speed in a mix master.

"Geez... I can hardly see." Edison struggled as the sand and vegetation were being caught up in a hellish vortex. "Oh my god..." muttered Edison, as he squinted and saw an unusual anomaly amongst the erratic lava formations and vegetation in the area. It was momentary.... In a depression on the sandy ocean floor was half of a rectangular box jutting out... its clearly squared off features against the natural rocks.... The same one he saw back at the lab in his vision...Then it was gone as fast as it appeared... covered by the swirling sand.

As Edison approached for a closer look, he noticed Tom, unconscious on the surface beginning to sink into the water... "That box could be buried forever if I don't...will Hack be better able to get Tom?"

Edison immediately inhaled deeply and stored as much air in his lungs as he could handle and kicked up to Tom grabbing him as he sank below the surface and took the regulator from his mouth and forced it into Tom's, while he struggled to get his arms around him to pull him back above the water.

As he was able to float with Tom in his arms on the surface, Edison was shocked by the eery quiet after the screeching and slamming of crushing metal hitting the surf and sinking through the water and hitting the bottom with such a thud and all the currents and the underwater sand storm created by the mass. What made it even more weird were the two voices, arguing with one another, while treading water.

"What in the hell is wrong with you."

"What the hell is wrong with me????"

"Are you insane?"

"Yeah…but I didn't quit… did I?

"Do you realize we could've been killed?

"Yeah… but I didn't quit…did I?

"Are you OK?

"Yeah… I think so… everything seems to be working."

"Except your brain…"

"You OK?"

"Yeah… let's get back to shore… I'm going to have to call your mother…what the hell am I going to tell her… oops, we had an unfortunate accident?"

"Don't worry Pop… we'll figure something out."

"Your mother is gonna kill me…. You know that don't you?

"Let's tell her together… maybe if she sees us in the same room not killing each other, she may not get mad…"

"Yeah… she sure would like that, I guess…"

"Are you two OK... is anyone hurt?" screamed Robin as she swam to the crash site.

"What the hell are you doing here... did Mom put you up to this?" Harley asked

"Hey Hon... Nice of you to show up, but everything's under control."

"Yeah... I can see that you two morons. I was watching from the shore." Robin retorted. "Where's Tom... is he OK?"

"I've got him here.... He's been knocked out, but I don't see any blood or anything...he's breathing." Edison yelled out as he slowly pulled him toward the shore. "I could use a hand..."

"Tom.... Tom are you OK? . ...Tom....Tom....!" Robin redirected her attention.

"Let's get him in and give him mouth to mouth." Edison offered.

"Hurry...Hurry..." Robin pleaded as they both grabbed an arm and swam toward the shore.

Fred and Harley were ahead, swimming almost at the shoreline,

Kate met them coming in....

"Tom.... Tommy..." She pleaded... with no response...

"I think he'll be OK, we just need to get him to shore, ASAP." Edison stated, huffing.

Kate grabbed his legs and began pulling.

CHAPTER 45

One Short

The first EMS ambulance was screaming down the road toward the point at Laupahoehoe Point Park.

"What's the situation?" asked the first EMS guy only half out of the passenger door?"

"We've got an unconscious guy here...no blood." Edison stated.

"Did he take in any water?"

"Maybe, but not much... I had the regulator on him most of the time."

"Good." Kimo....get the respirator!"

The EMS attendants worked on Tom for a few moments when up erupted whatever Tom had involuntarily swallowed out in the water... his eyes abruptly opened and his whole body jerked up and down.

"Easy guy... you're OK... do you know your name?"

Tom couldn't speak, but he nodded his head to let him know he had his faculties.

"We're going to take you to the hospital, just relax, everything should be OK.... You've got to relax ya ya."

Tom nodded his head again.

"Is there anyone else?"

Kate then realized..."Wait, where's the old guy out in the boat...has anyone seen him?"

Everyone shook their heads.

Kate immediately grabbed her flippers and her regulator and headed for the surf.
"I'll come with you..." Edison assured.

"We're going to take this one in, there should be two other ambulances here any time." Kimo said.
"I'll go with you." Robin stated emphatically.

The second ambulance arrived just as the first was leaving, both waving at each other as they passed.

"What's da story... what's goin on? Asked Saba.
"O Man.. don't tell me...Fred, you doin this? I shoulda known you two...not again.... You OK...? Saba knew the history of Fred and Harley.
The police cruiser was arriving. No one seemed injured, but Saba insisted that Fred and Harley go with them to the hospital to be checked..."Besides... you need a ride home, ya ya?"
The police officer asked what happened and Saba took him aside and briefly explained and suggested he talk with Fred and Harley at the hospital later. The officer chuckled, shook his head and agreed. "Any one hurt?"

"Everyone should be OK." Saba stated...Kimo took someone to the hospital but I think he'll be OK..."

"Stay here a moment while I look inside." Edison told Kate, who clung to the side of the boat, which had gouges in it... and blood splattered over it.

"The poor bastard...." Edison almost choked on his words."
"What?"
"Forget it, he's dead...." Edison informed her. "You don't want to look at it... it's pretty gruesome.... Let's get back to shore and let the EMS guys handle this."
They began swimming quietly back to the shore.

After a few minutes...
"Who's in the boat?" asked the officer.

"Some old guy... those two coming back went to check on him."
"From the look on your face, I'm guessing the guy in the boat didn't make it?" observed the officer.
"He's dead. Cut up pretty bad from the propeller blades." Edison informed.
"I'll call the coroner."
The third ambulance arrived and the officer spoke with them about the boat. Both attendants took their snorkels and swam out to the boat and pulled it back to shore.
They then pulled out a body bag and lifted Hack into it, loaded up the ambulance and drove away.

You guys need a lift?" The officer asked Edison and Kate?
"No, we have a car over there, we're OK."
"Get some rest and stop by the office in the morning, will you? I'll need a statement from each of you. I've got to get to the hospital now to file a report."

"OK…we'll be there…"

"I'll have the cranes come in tomorrow to dig those things out… not enough time left today." The officer observed. He pulled away.

Suddenly, after all the mayhem, the silence was deafening.

Edison and Kate just stared at each other.

Kate, said…" I really should get to the hospital to make sure Tom is OK, and if he is… I may kill him anyway."

"I'm sure he's OK, you might want to wait here just a few minutes while I check something out before all the heavy equipment gets here tomorrow."

CHAPTER 46

Be Careful What You Hope For

Edison and Kate swam out to the point where he saw the box half buried in the sand saw a corner sticking up at an acute angle from all the disruption of the helicopters on the floor. They dragged the battered box along with them to the shore and out of the surf at the farthest point of Luapahoehoe Point park. "This damn thing weighed a lot less in the water." He thought as Kate helped him pull the box further up the rock strewn shore area of the park.

The box measured roughly 18 inches by 10 inches and 6 inches high. It was originally painted green, but clearly had been in the surf for quite awhile, had become splintered, gouged, but yet still pretty much in-tact. The box was nailed with a curious type ornate headed nail on all four corners and four additional ones spaced evenly apart along the long sides of the box.

"Is that it?" Kate asked.

"I'm positive. This is really weird, but this looks like the same box I saw in one of my 'visions' back at the lab." Edison reported. A wave of emotion cascaded over his whole body as he realized this was the clear evidence that his theory that embedded memories of his parents were indeed recorded in his DNA at conception was probably true. "My God!" he thought to himself…. "It's true!… it's real!"

Edison began shaking. Kate placed her hands on his cheeks to calm him down a bit thinking Edison was referring the box of coins, but Edison didn't even give the box a moment's thought. All he could think about was his Ph.D. dissertation. "It worked. It's real. Damn!"

Edison and Kate finally sat down of one of the many rocks on the shoreline. This was not a swimming beach. It almost looked like the landing beach at Normandy with sharp irregular rocks jutting up, protecting it from any possible invaders. Edison was badly bruised from his jump and Kate was simply wiped out, physically and emotionally. No one was left on the beach. Everyone else had left. It was eerily quiet. They watched as the waves crash into the rocks and the white water swirling around... it was strangely soothing.

The view was becoming so spectacular and calming at the same time, that they briefly forgot about the box. A slight chill developed as they were both wet and a breeze picked up, typical at the point. Kate grabbed his arm and wrapped hers around his and gently squeezed and pulled him toward her, for warmth. Edison didn't fight it. Instinctively, Edison put his other arm around her head and drew her even closer. They gazed momentarily at each other's eyes. Edison had never noticed Kate had deep green eyes, which contrasted so beautifully with her dark hair.

Kate couldn't stop herself and firmly, without being too aggressive, kissed Edison on the lips.

After a few seconds of quiet affection, Edison pulled away.

"Oh God!" He exclaimed. "Evan... Mel" Edison began to utter, while...

Kate simultaneously uttered, "Melissa."

They pulled apart and the box was once again on center stage. They stared at it.

Edison thought of all the pirate stories he had read as a boy. He wondered what 'pirate' treasures were inside.

Edison slowly got up and commented, "Man am I going to be sore tomorrow." So far, he was still OK. He grabbed the all purpose fold up utility tool from the supply box, sat back down on the rock and began to pry open the nails holding the box lid secure to the frame. The nails were rusty and Edison was hoping for some WD-40 lubricant. The process went slow, but progress was made. One nail, partially removed, then another, another and so on until all eight nails had been loosened half way. Edison looked at Kate and they knew the time had come.

Whatever was inside would hopefully answer the lifelong questions Edison had about his father, whatever her father had spent the better part of his life, whatever Hack was looking for after all these years...

"Maybe there are bones in here instead of coins." He thought, as he momentarily hesitated in finally opening the box. "Let's get this over with, are you ready?" he asked Kate.

"Kate responded abruptly..."Did you say coins?... gold coins?"

"I think so... maybe..."

"That's why Tom is here, that's why Tom has been following us from Springfield... that's why he is so obsessed with this whole thing... THE CASE.... The fuckin' CASE. Pop, do you realize you almost got us all killed... over the fuckin' case!" she exclaimed looking up to the sky.

Kate shaking her head back and forth, nodded and both of them began to pull the nails out of the box by rocking them back and forth with their fingers, getting more sore with each nail... back and forth until they were all removed and the lid was indeed loosened. Edison opened up the knife portion of the tool and began to pry the lid open.

The inside of the box was divided into equal square sections, like an egg crate, each square area being about 1 ½ inches on each side. The dividers went as deep as the box itself. There were water soaked shreds of paper encrusted over the top of the box and there were also some of the dividers with the waxed paper still somewhat intact. Although there were a couple of dividers empty, the rest of them contained...

neatly stacked gold coins, some exposed, some still in a waxed wrapper kind of material...

"They're still shiny, like new." Edison exclaimed.

"Wow!" is about all Kate could muster.

Edison gently pulled one of the coins out of a divider.

On top it read, "UNITED STATES OF AMERICA" over "E PLURIBUS UNUM"

There was a flying eagle in the center and more sunshine with the words, "IN GOD WE TRUST" on the bottom.

Edison flipped the coin, and on the other side, it showed a walking Liberty with sunshine behind her. On top it read, "LIBERTY". The date was ..."1933".

"Whoa..." Edison uttered in disbelief. "These are the same coins I saw in the lab... the same ones I looked up in that coin book, based on what I saw."

"You're kidding, aren't you? Kate asked in amazement.

"Aah, no I'm not." "Do you realize how much each one of these are worth, based upon what the coin book said?"

"How much?" she asked now realizing this was like finding sunken treasure.

"If I remember correctly, each 1933 double eagle in uncirculated condition…"

"Well these certainly look uncirculated, they look brand new." Offered Kate.

"I think they were listed at $ 50,000 apiece!" and higher…and there must be over two hundred of these here."

"I'm not much at math, but you're talking $ 10 million dollars Edison!"

"Yep, that's what I figure, too," Edison quietly mumbled, his eyes glazed over.

"Could you actually take these to a coin dealer and get $ 10 million ?"

"I guess those prices are retail, but even so…" Edison thought.

"$10 million bucks!" Kate could hardly hold it in. "Does anyone actually own these things?" she asked.

"I think they were stolen from a train in the 1930's on the way to a Federal Reserve Bank, or whatever they had back then, but they never acknowledged they were stolen, because of the Great Depression, they didn't want to create any lack of confidence in the banking system, so I think they just wrote them off." "FDR issued an order to melt all the coins and have them all destroyed." These must be the only remaining 1933 gold coins left in existence.

"You mean no one is looking for these?" "No one today even knows they exist?"

"I'm sure someone must know something about these, but I doubt they would admit it. But for $10 mil, who knows?"

"What do we do?" Kate asked.

"This is one of those questions for Ethics 101." Edison observed.

"And just how ethical are we going to be?" Kate responded.

"I really don't know." Is this like found treasure? It's not ours, per se, unless you go with the possession is 9/10^{ths} of the law thing. If it's lost or abandoned, maybe we do own it."

"$10 million... $10 million... all at once..." Kate shook her head.

"Wait a second." Edison paused after listening to Kate's comment.

"What?" Kate asked.

"Well... even if each coin is worth $ 50,000, that means they must be very rare."

"Well, duh, yeah."

"Think about it... I may not be an economic guru, but if we were to dump all these on the market at once, they wouldn't be so rare anymore ...and the price would drop... maybe a fraction of the listed price in the book... the book listed these coins as rare because there were so few known ones... now...

CHAPTER 47

Case Closed

Tom was sitting at his desk, a bit drained from his meeting with Captain Hughes. Tom was not accustomed to getting chewed out by his superiors... he had always been a model cop, but going AWOL on a personal mission might work in the movies for Eddie Murphy, but not in real life.

Tom was grasping the several folders, some old, some faded, some torn, some new, some thick, some thin. Tom pulled out a picture of his father, Ernie in his full uniform. Tom slid the picture in the top folder, which was old, faded and creased. He then wrapped a rubber band around the folders.

Tom pulled out a rather large rubber stamp, inked it up on a pad of red ink, he stared at the bottom to make sure there was enough ink on the stamp and shook his head and in one fluid motion, stamped the pile of file folders on top, "CASE CLOSED".

He carefully folded up the ink pad and put both back into his desk drawer.

Tom put his first two fingers of his left hand to his lips, and then gently pressed them on top of the stack of files. As he held his fingers on the folders, his right hand assumed a full salute as he sat up straight, looking upward.

"Bye Pop... This one's for you!"

CHAPTER 48

Back to Paradise

Tom had just finished his shift and was getting his coat from his locker. There were about ten officers milling about in between shifts.

One of them, Chip, a sergeant, walked up to Tom and asked, "How did it go with the Captain?"

Tom responded, "Aaaah, it coulda been worse, I guess. Looks like I'll be getting an official reprimand on my permanent record. Thankfully is did relate to a local case."

"Yeah, I guess it could've been worse, I mean going AWOL without permission, well…at least you got a tan…. And I could think of worse places than Hawaii. Was it worth it?"

"I don't know. On one hand I'm glad this mess is over with. On the other hand, I don't think we'll ever know everything that happened. I just hope my old man isn't rolling over in his grave… He really wanted this thing solved.

"I remember ol' Ernie. I'm sure he's proud of you. You gave it all you could." He stated as he put his arm briefly around Tom and patted him on the back.

"Let me know if there's anything I can do for you." he added.

"Thanks, I'm just going to head over to my Mom's and have dinner with her… and I'll have to figure out something else to obsess over, from now on."

Richie saw Tom and went over to him. "Hey slick, you got a letter. Desk Sergeant asked me to give it to you, here." "Oooh, it's from Hawaii. And it looks like a woman's handwriting." He taunted.

Chip jokingly chimed in, "Gee, with that kind of detective work, Richie, you should be getting your gold badge, just about any decade now, eh?… What an eye."

"Looks like you found a hula honey while you were there?"

Richie and Chip started swinging their hips in jest.

Tom observed, "You guys better not quit your day job, really. I'm outta here."

With that, Tom looked a bit surprised when he buttoned up his coat, but he was in such a hurry to get out of there and read his letter, he didn't pay any attention to it and left while Chip and Richie were mimicking hula dancers, "Oooooh a ooooooh!"

Tom slid the letter in his right coat pocket and hurried out of the precinct.

On one hand, he was anxious to see what Robin was writing to him about and yet he was in no hurry to open it. He was just happy holding on to the letter, for the time being, basking in the uncertainty of what was in the letter. His hopes were better than reality for the time being and that was OK by him.

Tom's mother was cooking some pasta and chicken as he began to take off his coat, again feeling the smoothness of the letter from Robin. He then noticed something else in his pocket, but much more rigid.

"Are you hungry, Tom?" Mom asked.

"Yeah, ma, just give me a minute upstairs to clean up, OK?"

"OK, hurry up while it's still hot."

Tom was shocked. He stood, eyes wide open and jaw dropped almost to the floor as he pulled out a thin plastic sleeve with four filled pockets from his sport coat.

He just stared at the clear plastic sleeve he just pulled from his coat pocket. It weighed about a quarter pound, as he tossed it in his hands several times, holding it up to the light, staring at the reflection.

He just shook his head as he somehow walked out the upstairs bathroom and stood there for a few minutes.

After several moments, mom yelled up, "Tom, are you OK, dinner's on the table, hon."

Tom came out of the bathroom and into his mother's room. He had just taken the plastic sleeve with four pockets and slipped it into the box she kept with Ernie's medals and commendations in her bureau.

Tom contemplated, "This is sooo perfect!"

Dinner was sweet. Tom didn't say much. He just kept smiling. Mom knew after years with Ernie, that his mind was running on about something important and probably best not to interrupt. Dinner was sweet. Very sweet.

Later that night at home, Tom sat in front of his computer and closed all of the surveillance windows that he had been staring at on his desktop these past weeks. He finally pulled out the letter from Robin. He passed it through his fingers several times and then ever so slowly, opened it... unfolding it... and reading it... hanging onto every word. He smiled. He re-read the letter. He smiled some more. He read it a third time.

Tom picked up his mouse and typed on the keyboard and looked at his calendar, marked with his vacation weeks.

Tom continued typing,

FROM:....BDL
TO:..........ITO

CHAPTER 49

Even Hack Gets His Due

Roger Elam looked at the clock. 11 PM. He was tired and it was time for bed. He had just been released from the hospital that afternoon and he was looking for a good night's sleep without being interrupted every couple hours by the nurses or the other patients. He was exhausted and deflated after learning the news about his father.

He got up slowly from his chair with great difficulty, clutching his cane. He remembered he had to get his toothbrush from the manila envelope marked "PERSONAL EFFECTS". He thought, "It must be in there, that envelope was pretty heavy, I hope they put it in there."

He carried the envelope into the bathroom, leaned up against the counter and began to tear open the envelope.

He first pulled out his car keys and lamented to himself, "Well, I won't be able to use these anymore. I wonder how much I'll be able to get for that old rusty bucket?" Not realizing Hacks's blue Caddy was still at the Pittsburgh International Airport Long Term Parking and tossed them into the corner.

He next pulled out some papers, glanced at them and seeing there was nothing urgent tossed them on the counter, off to the left of the sink.

He then found his toothbrush and small tube of toothpaste and pulled both out relieved that he would be able to brush his teeth.

The envelope was still heavy and at first glance, he couldn't see anything else inside. He shook the envelope upside down.

There was a clear plastic sleeve with six pockets. He looked at the back of six coins firmly inside each pocket.

"UNITED STATES OF AMERICA"
"E PLURIBUS UNIM"
with an eagle flying over
"IN GOD WE TRUST"
They looked golden.
He flipped them over, a walking Liberty
The date was 1933.

CHAPTER 50

What Goes Around...

A YEAR LATER . . .

It was Evan's first birthday, almost one year after the Hawaiian adventure and Edison was in his study, gazing at the single shiny $20 1933 Gold St. Gaudens Double Eagle coin retrieved from the shore at Laupahoehoe that he kept locked up in his small combination safe in the closet. Indeed, it was the forbidden fruit, but he just couldn't help but keep just one as a souvenir. After finding out that the coins were illegal to own and that it would literally be a Federal crime to hang onto them, he dutifully turned the remaining coins in at the local FBI office. The government in a rare moment of decency, being grateful to put a period at the end of the The Case, at least gave him the current value of the gold in all the coins, a rather hefty sum, although not anywhere near the millions that everyone had been maneuvering for in order to hit the grand slam, the big score of a lifetime.

After locking up the forbidden fruit, Edison slung himself over the couch in the living room with his feet propped up over the end of the love seat, strumming some unrelated chords on his guitar, gazing at his son, Evan, sitting in his crib.

The sun was pouring in the window and a slightly crisp autumn breeze caused an occasional chatter in the mini-blinds covering the upper half of the open double hung window. It was a Sunday morning and Edison could not have been in a better place... at peace... at home ... with his son ... nowhere to rush off to ... just his guitar and the background beat provided by Evan's hiccup... hiccup... hiccup.

"You've ...got ... them ... hicci-cup blues..." Edison started singing while trying to figure out a good chord progression. He decided on a slow bluesy progression.

E
"You've got them hicci cup blues,

I don't know just what to dooos,
B
About them hicci cup blues.....
You've got those hicci cup blues,
I don't know what to do
E
About those hicci cup blues..
A
Well, I don't know,
I really don't care,
E
You daddy's got you wearin Scooby-doo underwear
B
You've got those hicci cup blues
A
I don't know what to doos
E   Bflat7sustained
About them hicci, those hicci cup blues

Just as Edison was gaining some momentum, he cracked a smile… pleased with himself for creating this new top ten hit.

"Edison… you'd better not quit your day job." …came a female voice from the other room as a reality check.

"I'm going out to Gus and Paul's for the bagels… they should be coming out of the oven in about fifteen minutes and I'll be back in a half hour. Anything else you need while I'm out?" she asked.

"No. Everything's cool here." Edison responded. "Unless you feel like getting some guava juice. It might help the morning sickness."

"Good idea… now that you mention it, I'm not sure which will be coming out of the oven first… little Clark's really active today… just make sure Evan's changed by the time I get back so we can have brunch while the bagels are still warm, OK?" she asked.

"Consider it done. Edison replied.

"Once she comes out, you know we're going to have to come up with a real name."

As Edison heard the door close, he left his guitar on the couch, walked over to Evan's crib and as he picked him up, held him close to his face and looked him straight in the eyes, rubbed noses and said,

"OK EB, now we're really going to have some fun!" "Just wait for your sister to get here!"

THE END

EPILOG

The next day when Edison arrived home after work, he found a letter from New England Federal Bank & Trust, Springfield, MA.

Dear Mr. Barr,

We are pleased to inform you that recently we became aware of an inactive managed trust account wherein you are the named beneficiary opened in 1965...

STARRING ROLES

Edison:
A late 30's owner of a music store who grew up never knowing his father. He is now about to have his first child with Melissa and is confronted with threats from Harry Elam wanting information about the whereabouts of valuable gold coins supposedly involving his father, but his mother, Dorothy has secrets and refuses to tell him anything about his father. Edison finds himself in a situation where he must engage in a risky attempt to access his DNA as a means to acquiring information about his father as a last resort to protect his family.

Will:
A late 30's best childhood friend of Edison, who also grew up without a father in his life. Will is a Ph.D. in Computer Science and finds someone spying on Edison online. Will is the only person that can relate with Edison about growing up without a father.

Melissa:
A 30's medical doctor managing a team of researchers doing research on knowledge acquisition, retention and transfer using lab rats in mazes. She is having her first child with Edison, but refuses to get married. She can be clinical, sarcastic and not the warmest person in the room, but is intelligent and committed to Edison until threatened by Harry Elam.

Kate:
A 30's member of Melissa's research team who is developing strong feelings for Edison, fully aware of her unrequited love and the untenable situation she is in.

Tom:

Ernie Dugan's son who is following in his father's footsteps and becomes a Detective in the Springfield Police Department just like his dad and makes a promise to solve The Case, no matter what, after Ernie retires.

SUPPORTING ROLES

Artie: A 50ish black jazz musician from the 30's, playing in Pittsburgh. He has very gifted hands and is a new father.

Ernie: As a meticulous young detective on the Springfield Police Department, he got involved with a train robbery which hounded him for his entire career spanning 40 yrs. He never gave up, but never solved The Case. We see Ernie both young and old in his quest to solve The Case.

Harry: Harry 'Hacksaw' Elam was involved with the train robbery as a kid. He was the only one that went to prison for his involvement in the robbery. Thirty years later, after being paroled, he is looks for revenge against those who cut him out of his share of the robbery. We also see Harry even later in life He now has a pressing need for the robbery money and will stop at nothing to get his due.

Dorothy: Edison's loving mother with one exception. She refuses to tell him anything about his father. She has secrets.

Miss Louise: An elderly senior. She remembers Edison's father and shares her memories with him about life back in the 30's.

Dave: A member of Melissa's research team who finds out secrets about Edison's past and then helps him find the means to unlock the secrets of Edison's father's past.

para*Flix*®

You're the Producer! Read the brief description of each character on the previous pages and then cast the roles with actors [dead or alive] you wish to play these roles in order to bring *A Deja View* to life... for your own personal movie production... and hear their voices while you read and imagine the scenes while you experience this...

para*Flix*® DocuDrama

It's a new kind of book.

With **para*Flix*...** It's OK to hear voices!®

* = starring role

<u>Remaining roles are to be played by appropriate people as cameo appearances.</u>

Cast: **Played By:**

*1. **Edison:**_____
*2. **Will:**_____
*3. **Melissa:**_____
*4. **Kate:** _____
  5. **Tom:** _____
  6. **Ernie:**_____
  7. **Harry:**_____
  8. **Dorothy:**_____
  9. **Artie:**_____
 10. **Miss Louise:**_____
 11. **Dave:** _____

www.ingramcontent.com/pod-product-compliance
Lightning Source LLC
Chambersburg PA
CBHW071119170626
46809CB00002B/422